SPAGHETTI, MEATBALLS, & MURDER

A 2nd Chance Diner Mystery

BETH BYERS

For Kirsten and Daymon and Devon
and Joe and Kim and Pam and Shana and Stephanie
and Angie and Taryn and Christina and all those other
poor fools who made my own sedentary trip
through hell a little better

AUTHOR'S NOTE

There is not a beach town in Oregon named Silver Falls.
The other towns, however, exist and are delightful. Many of the other locations
I reference are real and were selected based entirely on my adoration.
Pick a lovely little town and go breathe some salty sea air.
You'll be better for it.

But it's the Oregon Coast. Bring a jacket.

C all center jobs are sedentary forms of safaris through hell. You're miserable *and* your butt is getting ever wider. It doesn't matter what company you work for—they're all bad. It all started when we had a fire alarm and a plumbing issue the same week at work.

The fire alarm was first. You'd think that First, the fire alarm went off. The doors closed to help control the fire. But then management blocked every exit, preventing people from leaving, while they *confirmed* the fire. And as MAD as that made me, I stayed at my desk and answered calls with the alarm blaring so loudly I had customers offer to hang up so I could get to safety. Sure, the reason it was going off was some idiot who'd combined popcorn and a microwave and done it poorly. But still...what if it hadn't been?

Two days later the sewage backed up. The toilets, sinks, and water fountains weren't safe to use. What did they do? They brought in portable potties and bottled water, but they didn't get a handicapped potty, and a co-worker was in a wheelchair. It was so far beyond enough that I found myself confused about *why* I was still there. So I got up, told the weirdo who sat across from me goodbye and did the long, slow, *sweet* walk of freedom.

There is something absolutely magical about dropping your bag over your shoulder and leaving a place you hated. I wouldn't have done it...I was supposedly responsible...but I just *snapped*. Maybe I wasn't acting responsibly. Or only semi-responsibly. Like people who get Bachelor's degrees in literature. Or people who pay their bills but spend too much on makeup. I had a savings account. I lived in a tiny, cheap, basement apartment. I'd be okay.

Perhaps it wasn't the sewage or the fire alarm that finally set me off. Maybe it was the way the moon was full, how the wind blew my hair that morning, and how it smelled like rain. Maybe it was the way I felt like ants were crawling under my skin every minute I spent chained to that desk. Or it was the way I was far too close to forty to be where I was in my life and it was entirely unsatisfactory.

The real prompter wasn't, of course, the smell of rain. I lived in the Pacific Northwest. It rained eight months straight every single year. If I had gotten a degree in Psychology instead of Lit, I might try to blame it on the death of my grandparents. I thought their deaths should have hit me harder than they had, but my mother had been estranged from them so I barely knew them. I'd gone to their funeral and heard about their passions and their friendships. I learned about their careers and spent the eulogy wondering how much of a disappointment I had been to them. That idea bothered me. But then... then...I had written in my journal and realized that their disappointment wasn't what bothered me. Mine was.

I was disappointed in myself and that feeling swirled up with the wind in my hair and the full moon and the scent of rain and made a mess inside me. All it took was the spark of backed-up sewage and a handicapped friend who needed to pee but couldn't.

And, I exploded.

"WHAT'S YOUR PLAN?" MOM ASKED WITHOUT AN EXPRESSION, OR the flicker of a lash, even though I'd abandoned my job. She'd actually laughed when I told her I walked out without a word. I was in this surreal land of madness where my incredibly responsible parent wasn't concerned that I was unemployed.

"I don't have a plan," I admitted, the need to be rational fighting with my desire to shout hurray that I'd escaped.

After I walked out of my job, I'd gone to my Mom's. She wasn't there. She probably had a meeting with a student or paused in the hallway outside her office to discuss *A Midsummer Night's Dream* with another professor. I'd waited with a mug of her luxurious cocoa and my journal, snuggled into my favorite of her chairs, and marveled at what I'd done.

I'd realized as I flipped through my journal how each passing page elucidated the feelings of the last years. I'd been so unhappy, I'd forgotten what peace felt like. I'd been so used to the monotony, so used to the idea of responsibility, and so focused on deliberately avoiding thinking too hard.

Leaving was my journal's fault, I realized. My journal and the magic of writing and the way I had faced my feelings. And what I wanted in life. I might not have a plan, but I had a dream.

My mom had come home as I started making pro and con lists for the future. The cons were far too many, but the singular pro was powerful. Happiness.

"Graduate school?" Mom asked. Her voice was a cool neutral, showing me how much she didn't want to sway my decision even though it had been her dream for me.

I tapped my journal. It was just a spiral notebook with a unicorn on it because it made me smile. Mom didn't know that while writing about my misery for all this time, I'd been trying to discover what made me excited. And what I found had been utterly unexpected.

"I don't want to go to graduate school," I said, quietly.

"What *do* you want?" Mom said it like it mattered, but we were adults. We both knew that what I actually wanted couldn't be switched on and off because wanting something didn't make it feasible.

I suppose it wouldn't hurt to tell her what I wanted. I never had. Not once. It wasn't that we weren't close. We were. It was just that she was a professor. I assumed that she'd smile before trying to talk me into graduate school. Again. But, this time I told her.

"You want a diner?" she asked.

I nodded, biting my lip. I didn't want to see her disappointment.

"At the beach?"

I nodded again.

It might be coming out of nowhere to her, but I'd been dreaming about this for a while. I'd learned to make meals for my dream diner and never told her why. I'd perfected a chocolate layer cake without explaining how I wanted it displayed in a string of beautiful, funky dome-covered cake plates along the top of a glass counter. I learned to make pie and ice cream and cinnamon rolls and biscuits with gravy. I'd perfected chicken fried steak and hash browns and french fries. I'd drawn pictures of booths with fun chandeliers and pretty wood floors and never, not once, told my mom what I'd wanted.

"It won't happen," I said, knowing it was true. It was what I had been saving for, but I didn't have enough. I probably never would. "But that's what I want. It's hard to figure out anything else when this is it."

A diner. Simple food,recipes, feeding people, the smell of the ocean, a small town without corporations. I didn't want to hear about shareholders ever again.

"Really?"

My expression must have reflected what I thought of her continued surprise.

"It isn't what I pictured," she said. Her short hair fell into her face and an emotion crossed her expression that I couldn't quite read.

"It's not going to happen," I repeated defensively. "But I'm tired of wanting it and not doing anything. I'm thinking, I'll take my savings and try to find a little apartment and a job. Maybe in Astoria or Lincoln City. It'll be better than misery in the call center."

"Rosemary—"

"I don't want to disappoint you," I cut in, "but I can't keep living like this. I'm sorry. Having a waitress daughter at the beach was never what you wanted."

"Rosemary Desdemona Elizabeth Baldwin," Mom snapped, "you have never disappointed me. I don't understand why you didn't tell me."

"I know," I said, wishing I'd been brave enough to tell her. Maybe brave enough to pursue what I wanted before.

"I am not a snob," she continued. "I teach at a community college, not at Harvard. All I want is for you to be happy. It's all I ever wanted."

"I know..."

"Just because I love talking about Shakespeare and Jane Austen doesn't make me think that other things are stupid."

"I know..." I felt like I was thirteen again and hated feeling like that.

"If making cinnamon rolls will make you happy, I think you should do it. And having your own place, I could see why that would be important to you."

"I can't," I snapped. "I wish it were possible, but I don't have enough saved."

"Oh, Rose..." Mom bit her lip and examined my face for too long before she said, "You know I've been dealing with so much. I—"

"Your mom and dad died," I said with a watery sniff. "This isn't your fault. I snapped at work. And I *am* an adult. I should be acting responsibly."

"We weren't close," Mom pushed on, ignoring my interruption. "You know that. But I knew—"

"I'm sorry to bring this up again," I said cutting in again. I took my mom's hand. It was so unfair. I had such a great parent and she had so much less. "I don't want to make things harder for you. None of this is fair to you."

"Rosemary, my love..." Mom shook her head and reached out and smacked me lightly on the side of my head. "Let me finish. Because, you darling fool, I got a call from my parents' lawyer."

I leaned back, trying to read her face. She was struggling to speak.

"I *knew* they had money. But I didn't know what they'd do with it. Especially given how things were. But, goodness. They left everything to you and me. They split it equally and put it in trusts. They had a lot. And there will be more from the life insurance."

I had taken a swallow of cocoa, and I froze, holding it in my mouth.

"They were quite wealthy."

I blinked.

"Now we're quite wealthy. You could have a diner or a hotel or a house or never work again. I mean, I knew they had money, but not like this. And now it's ours."

Which is when what she was saying struck me and I choked on the feeling of my heart in my throat and the liquid in my mouth and coughed that luxurious cocoa all over my cream call center cardigan.

ACCORDING TO MY MOTHER, LIFE ON THE OREGON COAST REQUIRED a Subaru Forrester. I wasn't sure I agreed, but when she insisted I get a car, and I let the purchase happen. I wanted to more see if it *would* happen and verify I really did inherit money from my grandparents. Mom knew me well enough to know she was railroading me, and I was testing this surreal dream. When she was done, I had a shiny blue Forrester and a confirmation that money truly had come out of nowhere.

While I sorted my apartment, my mom barged in, picked up my laptop, and found me a cottage on the Oregon Coast for the next six months.

"Mom, I can do that."

"I'm excited," she said, tucking her hair behind her ear. "This is your dream. I can't wait to see it play out."

Even after the Forrester, I didn't believe it was real until Mom dragged me into the bank and had me sign more paperwork than I'd have thought necessary for anything but becoming the leader of the free world. When it ended, I was left speechless at the balances of the accounts, and the fact that people who had barely known me left it to me.

Mom was the one who started loading my new car. I helped, of course, but I got distracted by the scent of rain and the way the wind seemed to whisper happiness. Somehow, even as excitement bubbled in my stomach, finding my dream had become the most terrifying thing that had ever happened to me.

Mom put the last of my stuff into the Forrester and then squeezed me again. She looked at my face, cupped my cheeks and whispered, "Get a pet, find a lover, follow your dream, and drown in happiness. I'm not coming until you're settled. I want to see it in its glory, so get it together."

"*You* find a lover," I said, pulling back with a laugh.

Her glance to the side gave me pause. There was a twitch at the corner of her mouth, and I gasped, "You *have* a lover."

Mom's wicked grin told me I was right. What an idea! I was going to let her happiness carry me into my second chance. My hands shook as I started the car and backed out of the driveway. It was all beginning, and I was still waiting to wake up.

A fierce need to use the restroom had me stopping at the feed store outside of Silver Falls. I knew I wasn't that far from the cottage, but I hadn't been there before, and I didn't want to have an episode that only toddlers would empathize with.

I ran into the store, interrupted the store clerk, and wove my way through the aisles to the bathroom. When I finished, I decided to wander the store. What was it that made you feel guilty for using the restroom and not buying something? I had to at least pretend to look around. As if I would fool anyone.

The first aisle was animal food. The next was nails and hammers and other implements I tried to avoid. The one after that took me to an outdoor area where they were selling chicks and other baby birds. I paused to coo at them and then wandered past a desk where I heard little growls and yelps.

"Oh, hello," I said, squatting down to look closer at a pile of basset hound puppies in a cardboard box. There were, perhaps, a half dozen sets of floppy ears, wagging tails, and little black noses.

"They're fifty bucks," said a little boy with dark brown hair and bright blue eyes. "Mom said to get money for them so they don't get fed to snakes. They're full bred. It's a real, real good deal."

Too good of a deal, I thought. But one set of dark, soulful eyes caught mine and I knew I'd regret not at least petting the little soul. I lifted a puppy with each hand and felt two little noses brush against each of my cheeks, but the puppy in my right hand licked me frantically, and I couldn't help but put down the second puppy to snuggle my little lover.

"They're mutts."

It was a man's voice that cut into my puppy kisses. He was behind me, and his voice was enticingly deep and dark enough that I had to turn to see if his face matched it.

I suppose I stared because I'd expected a gut and a crooked nose. Something that was the complete opposite of that voice. What I got was a healthy man with dark stubble on his face, kind dark brown eyes, and a strong jaw. He wasn't stop you in your tracks handsome, but he was good looking. He had to be well over six feet tall. What also caught my attention was the way the boy's eyes lit up with sheer, unadulterated joy to see him.

The man continued speaking while I stared. "And JJ Masterson, your mom told you to make sure they found good homes and not to charge a single penny."

The boy's initial reaction was followed by a flush. "Fifty dollars is enough for the new Lego X-Box game," he moaned, "and this lady would have paid it. Look at her, 'Tective. She's a softy."

The man grinned and his passable attractiveness morphed into a long, tall drink of oh-my-goodness handsome.

"Hello," I said, grinning because I had no self-control, and he was just so handsome with that smile. "Thanks for saving me fifty dollars."

"You gonna take that puppy?" he asked. "They look like basset hounds, but Kat Masterson's female isn't a full breed. She'd be furious with her son for saying the dog was purebred."

The puppy wriggled as if it knew its future was on the line, kissing my cheek and laying its chin on my shoulder.

"I do feel like I've been chosen. I'm not sure I can leave, um—" I checked the sex, "—her behind." She had red ears and little red freckles on her nose, and her wrinkly, floppy skin was so soft. Her sweet puppy breath, and a few more kisses, and things were looking up.

The man grinned, showcasing a handsome set of teeth and making my knees weaken. I was easy. I had been too long in a call center full of people warped by their work. "You from around here?"

I scrunched my nose, told myself to make friends and not freeze up because he was handsome and *talking to me*. "I hope to be, but I'm moving here from Gresham. I'm staying in a little rental right now and figuring things out."

There was a warmth in his eyes that I hadn't seen for quite some time and I certainly hadn't expected. I tucked my hair—my frizzy, reddish hair—behind my ear and wondered how I looked after the drive. Given that I'd rolled the windows down and let the wind push me along, I suspected I looked a little bit homeless.

The flash of his grin said that he liked my answer, and I could feel my face heat in response to the way his gaze roved over me. Mostly my face, a level of tact I appreciated, since I was a bit thick from too much time literally tied to a phone and a chair.

"Now, JJ," he said, glancing at the boy. "Tell us about these pups."

JJ told me that my puppy was the one who liked to snuggle and had been sleeping by his shoulder every single night. Her best friend was a little fellow with darker ears and freckles.

The man the kid had called 'Tective held out his fingers to my little gal's freckled brother. What could 'Tective mean? Was it some weird nickname? Like the things people called each other while they were playing video games?

My puppy's little buddy waggled his tail and yipped at the man frantically. He jumped with so much excitement that he fell out of the cardboard box and began circling 'Tective's boot before JJ could catch him.

"Uh-oh," I said, wondering if he'd succumb. He put his hands on very lean hips as the puppy yipped at him again, touching him lightly with a paw—all the while, the puppy's tail was wagging so frantically it beat a tattoo against the ground.

The man looked over at me, grinned again—further weakening my knees—and scooped the pup up.

Was it gratuitous for an attractive man to stand there smiling at me with a puppy in his arms? There was something illicit about watching a tall, handsome man holding a wriggling, yipping puppy. Regardless of who this fellow was, this moment of watching him semi-flirt over a puppy belly had made this day perfect.

"I'm Simon Banks," he said, scratching the puppy's belly.

"Rosemary Baldwin," I replied and scratched his puppy's belly as a sort of adjusted handshake.

"I know you're new around here, but maybe you've seen the signs for the jazz festival happening in the park tonight. You going?"

I hesitated, wondering if he was asking me out, and then took the risk. "I hadn't heard about it, but that does sound fun."

"Maybe you'd like to join me for a picnic?"

I blinked. He *was*. He was *asking me out*. I liked the kindness in his eyes and the way he scratched that puppy's belly and the way the kid was looking at Simon as if he were a hero.

"That sounds lovely," I answered in a smooth, confident voice that definitely did *not* belong to me. "I need to get situated, but I should be able to make it."

"Great," he said. He glanced me over again, took note of the little red and white basset puppy in my hands and asked, "Need the puppy aisle?"

I grinned and followed, unashamedly enjoying the view from behind. Shopping for my new, little friend made my second chance seem all the more real, far more so than the car had. Maybe because the car had been at my mom's insistence and the puppy was all me. I found her a pink collar with white daisies on it, a leash and a name tag, dog bowls, and a few toys to chew on.

On the way out, I dug into my pocket and pulled out $50 for the child. These puppies hadn't been free to take care of, and I was betting his mom would have eventually bought him that game. I wanted to help at least some because I was thoroughly in love.

Simon noticed but said nothing. He did, however, walk me all the way to my car and opened the back for me. "His mom did tell him to give those puppies away."

I grinned as I confessed, "The boy is a charming scamp. And the puppies cost them money to care for."

Simon laughed. "Jay was right. You are a softy."

I shrugged because what else could I say?

His voice deepened, and I had to pause in sheer appreciation as he said, "I'm glad you're moving here, Rosemary."

"Me too." Suddenly feeling like an idiot, I wasn't quite sure what to do with my hands, and my hips were four sizes bigger than they had been a few moments before and somehow my feet were clownishly large.

"Are you going to work from home? Or did you get a job here? You looking?"

I hadn't told anyone but my mom what my plans were. It took me a moment to gear up my courage. "I'm planning to open a diner or perhaps a coffee shop."

My little puppy licked me and wriggled in my arms as if she approved. Or maybe she sensed how stressed it made me admit my dream, which sounded so insane. It was like saying you wanted to make a living by painting portraits—unlikely. Businesses like the one I was talking about failed all the time.

"Are you now? Have you been to Jenny's?"

I shook my head, hoping this wasn't some friend who already had an awesome diner and wouldn't like my plans.

"She's looking to sell. Has been for a while. You might check her out."

"Really?" I felt a thrill of hope that I could actually get my dream up and running. Maybe very soon.

Simon nodded. "She's on Main Street right next to the Soda Shoppe. Seems like a good spot for a restaurant to me. Now if you buy that place..." he paused dramatically, "I'm going to need to keep finding cinnamon roll pancakes for breakfast."

"I might be able to do that," I said, knowing cinnamon roll pancakes would be going on the official menu. What could be better than somewhere that was already established? I was getting super excited at the idea. Maybe I'd be pouring out pancakes and experimenting with the recipes that I was still working on in a week or two.

How long did it take to buy a diner if it was the right one for me? I could always slowly update it to match my dream. That might even be better if it were a well-loved place. My mind was racing, and my heart was thudding, and I was so excited I wanted to bounce, but I didn't want to look like a child.

"I'll have to check it out," I said, trying to keep my cool. "So where's the festival?"

"In the park next to the beach. Meet you by the Sacajawea statue. Seven tonight?"

I grinned and nodded and opened the passenger door of my car. I'd bought the puppy a bed, and I placed it on the passenger seat and put her in her new place. When I stood, he shut the door and walked me around the car to open the driver's side for me with the other puppy on his forearm.

"It was a pleasure to meet you, Rosemary," Simon said.

He did that grin again. I suppose it had been too long since I'd had attention from anyone. Which wasn't quite true, I just hadn't been that interested in anyone who'd made overtures before now.

"Likewise," I told him, hoping that meeting a gentleman before I'd even reached my new hometown was a sign of good things to come.

MY RENTAL WAS ONE IN A SET OF COTTAGES. THEY SURROUNDED A courtyard on three sides with the parking lot on the final side. The shared yard had a play set, a picnic table, and several benches. Each cottage had weathered, repurposed layered shingles. With bright doors and white shutters and flower boxes, the cottages were especially adorable given how the flower boxes and garden beds were full of color and greenery.

I walked through the little place with my puppy under my arm. The cottage was barely larger than a studio apartment, but it had things no college apartment would have: a large soaking tub, a separate shower, a wide cushy chair, and a fireplace. And the view was breathtaking. I had one of the cottages with the backside pointed toward the ocean, and the wide picture window off the living space showcased the crashing ocean and gray skies. The Oregon Coast might not be warm or conducive to sunbathing, but it was shockingly beautiful.

The living area had a small kitchen and eating nook, and a bedroom connecting to the big bathroom. The bedroom wasn't much bigger than the bed and an armoire, but it was lovely in shades of gray and green. The living room had a couch, the comfy chair facing the ocean, and a flat screen TV over the fireplace.

There was also a fenced back deck with a four-person hot-tub, a tiny patch of grass just big enough for the pup to do her business, and a small gas grill.

My puppy enjoyed every second running around, barking at anything that moved – in between marking her territory, but she stayed surprisingly close to me. Her floppy ears begged me to caress them, so I paused from unpacking my car long enough to play with her.

It wasn't until I started folding my clothes to put them away that I realized I didn't want those old things to contaminate my new life. I didn't want my call center khakis or the threadbare cardigans I'd worn year-round to hang in the tiny armoire.

I took out a plaid shirt I'd worn often. Working in the call center had given me a wider bottom and a bigger chest, and the shirt hadn't fit right for some time, but I'd worn it anyway. I threw it on over a tank and added lip gloss and a slapped dash of eyeshadow, not caring too much how I looked. Not anymore. Instead of putting my clothes away, I ruthlessly culled them and found myself left with a tiny pile of clothes that I didn't despise.

Was I being frivolous to decide to get new things? I couldn't help but wonder what my mom would think. She would, I realized, rub her hands together in sheer, unadulterated joy and make a comment about how it was long overdue. That clinched it. Plus, I rationalized wickedly, shopping would be a great way to check out the town. Ensure that this was where I wanted to live. We'd done enough research to know that Silver Falls was a booming town for tourism, similar to Cannon Beach or Leavenworth. It pulled in visitors with the sheer quaintness. Double checking what we'd researched while I shopped would be useful *especially* if I swung by Jenny's Diner and tried it out as a customer instead of a potential buyer.

I dug through the cabinets in the cottage until I found garbage bags and ruthlessly shoved my rejects in before dragging them to my car.

"So, puppy…"

She yipped at me.

"Want to go shopping?"

She jumped up, putting her paws on my shin, tongue lolling, and I scooped her up and let her lick my chin.

"Did you want a name?"

Her reply was a wriggling bottom until she was able to put her paws over my shoulder and nuzzle my neck.

I took inspiration from her collar. "How about Daisy?"

She nuzzled her nose into my neck. I took that as acceptance and clipped on her leash.

Silver Falls was small enough that we could walk from the cottage to the downtown area. As we did, moving slowly as Daisy sniffed everything and tested the length of her leash, I took deep breaths of salty sea air and had to acknowledge how very much I was enjoying being free from corporate life. I felt as if someone had taken shackles from my ankles, and a part of me was terrified I was about to be caught and hooked back up.

We paused while Daisy did her business for approximately the 70th time and as we did, I tucked my hair behind my ear, letting my head fall back and my eyelids go red in the sunlight. I took in a deep breath and wondered yet again, was this really happening?

A door slammed nearby, shocking me out of my daydream. I rubbed my eyes and glanced around, but I couldn't see where it had come from. Perhaps it was only the wind slamming a door shut, given the way it was whipping through town, but a moment later I heard, "Are you kidding me? You think I don't know what this is about? You think I don't know what kind of person you are?"

I didn't want to glance around, but the girl—whose voice was distinctly feminine—was yelling. And it was small-town life right? Snooping is what people did. I glanced towards the shouting and saw a curvaceous girl with a dark ponytail and a green dress uniform get into a small hatchback and peel away from the curb. She was coming far too fast, so I scooped Daisy up and stepped quickly back. I could see tears on her tan face. The distress was so distinct that I had to say a quick prayer there wouldn't be an accident given how emotional she was.

"Poor kid," I told Daisy. I thought about how fast the girl had been driving and added, "Poor, stupid kid."

❧ 3 ❧

I shopped until I was loaded down with bags. If getting a new wardrobe was any indication of how my new life was going to go, it would be expensive but super, super cute. I followed up by leaving my dog and bags at my rental and returning to eat at Jenny's. The Jenny in question was ancient. She wore orthotics, had thin hair, cat-eye glasses, and walked with a slight limp. Her food, however, was amazing. I ordered my favorite diner food that I rarely indulged in—chicken fried steak, mashed potatoes, gravy, and steamed broccoli. My stomach was pushing out over the top of my pants when I added the apple crumb pie.

Her staff was a woman nearly as old but twice as sprightly and the young girl who'd driven far too quickly. That girl didn't have a trace of the emotions she'd been carrying earlier on her face, and she was quick to refill my glass, deliver the food, and chatter about the town.

I asked her about the diner itself, somewhere to get my hair done, and how long she'd lived in town. She answered, but kept moving, somehow making it seem like she wasn't snubbing you while still doing her job.

Tara, the diner girl, suggested the Ocean Breeze Spa for a hair

salon. I figured I'd be able to get news as well as a new cut, so I w
there after eating. I added color and a mani-pedi to keep the gossip
coming. And I learned a *lot*.

Jenny's Diner was a huge favorite of the town and the best place for
brunch. The woman who owned it had opened it decades ago when
Silver Falls had been tiny. There were people who lived in town who
were as likely to have breakfast there every day as they were to have
breakfast at home. She couldn't sell the diner because no one was
willing to keep the staff on without question. Plus, with the precarious
financial times, a diner at the beach was risky for anyone.

"That's a sweet little thing in your lap," my stylist, Mattie, said
referring to Daisy.

"Isn't she?" It took me a moment to gather up my courage. "I got
her from a kid named JJ Masterson at the feed store. A real tall guy
from around here got one too. He was really nice. You're all so
friendly."

The stylist was no fool, and she winked at me. "Gotta name?"

I grinned at that wink. "Simon. Super tall. Dark hair. Dark eyes."

"Lovely build," she added. *"Simon*, the delicious. Good guy. A cop."

Aw. *That* explained the 'Tective.

"He grew up here," Mattie continued. "Went away to school, and
came back to be a cop. Most would tell you he's a playboy, but he's my
friend, and he's not a playboy. He's not fickle...he *is* a good guy. He just
hasn't settled down and everyone keeps expecting the next person he
dates to be *the* one. Makes him edgy."

"You said he was a good guy twice," I said, thinking *red flag*. The
idea of avoiding him was deflating my perfect day.

Mattie shook her head. "No, he really is a good guy. But don't get
ahead of yourself with him. He plays straight. Don't read into everything. Or anything."

I shifted enough that Mattie was able to tell that Simon and I
already had plans. She leaned down, taking my shoulder gently, and
said, "Really. He *is* a good guy. He's my friend."

Okay, I thought, okay. I scrunched up my nose. "Just have fun,
right?"

"Yes," Mattie said, adding, "Simon has been my friend since third grade so I can tell you that you'll have a good time. Also, your hair looks amazing even if I did do it myself." She ran her fingers through it. "I haven't had so much fun in a while."

"It's amazing what happens," I said dryly, "when someone gives you free rein. Now make it look like it wasn't done for a date."

She laughed, mussing it. "Jazz festival? Simon's a huge fan."

I nodded. She pulled back the top of my hair, putting it into sort of messy half-bun. She sprayed the rest and tousled it to hide the sharp edges. I doubted it would disguise that I'd gotten my hair done, especially if he was a *cop* and even semi-observant, but at least it made it seem like less of a big deal.

The last time my hair was cut I'd done it myself in the bathroom.. The time before that I'd made my mom do it, and she'd had two glasses of wine before she dared my wrath if she screwed up. The wine was reflected in the cut.

"The way to his heart is food," Mattie told me as she talked me into product after product for my hair. Not that I'd know how to use most of them.

"You stop it," I said, taking the bag from her, adding it to my other bags. "Thank you."

"I'll see you soon," Mattie said with another wink, "That color is best kept up at least every 4-6 weeks."

"You're a clever businesswoman, Mattie," I told her.

Her grin was pure naughty as she saw me out the door. "I'll call you for my next girl's night. I feel like you'll fit right in."

DAISY AND I WALKED BACK TO THE COTTAGE, AND I DUMPED THE bags on the bed. I had never spent more money in a day except for the day I'd bought the Forrester. I fed the puppy before examining my look in the mirror. I was wearing a favorite pair of jeans and the funky tank and a new plaid shirt, but I knew I had better change. An outside jazz festival next to the beach meant wind, dampness, and a chill that would sink into bones and make the event miserable even if the music was amazing.

I changed into a long-sleeved shirt, a new, pretty cardigan and topped everything with my blue coat. I put on boots that laced and looked amazing with my jeans. Somehow my call center-widened butt looked good in those jeans and the boots accentuated that even more. I had fun with my makeup, trying to avoid going full glam even though it was so fun when I did.

Finally, I added a pretty scarf I'd found in a little yarn shop. The shop owner told me they had a knitting circle for 'all levels,' so I'd taken the information. I decided to go even though I couldn't knit and had never wanted to knit. What I wanted were friends and connections in this town.

As I walked toward the festival my mind was wandering. I *loved* Jenny's Diner and already renamed it in my head. My decoration ideas were brewing and I'd even found a perfect cake plate, as though someone had crafted it straight out of my imagination. I should probably shop around to compare diners given this was my dream and a *huge* investment. But I wasn't going to. If I could make Jenny's happen, I'd wire transfer the money tomorrow. Going inside had felt like coming home. It even had the glass cabinet of my dreams. All that it was missing were my cake plates and trays of cinnamon rolls, chocolate cake, cookies, and muffins, but I could fix those things easily.

I glanced over to the diner as I passed it. It *was* lovely. I stopped to take stock again and felt hope rising even higher in my heart. The building was brick and there were bay windows on either side of the double doors. It had been created with the artisanship that came from earlier times. Both bay windows had little tables set off from the rest of the diner, giving the illusion of privacy.

I could envision wood flooring instead of the linoleum that hadn't aged well. Reupholster booths in updated colors. Maybe some—

A loud squeal broke me out of my thoughts. I glanced around, trying to figure out where the noise was coming from.

Oh my...no! A car was coming right at me. More instinct than reason had me jerking back. I fell, yanking Daisy by her leash onto my chest as my head hit the ground. I heard a shriek and a crunch, but my head was ringing too much from where it had slammed into the cement, so I wasn't sure what was happening.

Whines filled the air, and it took far *too* long to realize it was Daisy. I tucked her close to my chest. I could feel her kisses and the wriggles of her body and thought she must be okay. It was then that I tried and failed to push myself up. I rubbed my forehead and then tried again. My elbow and rear were aching, and the puppy was pawing at me. This was a beach town where the speed limit was 20 miles an hour. I'd eat my new coat if that car hadn't been going at least twice that. Maybe three times.

"Are you all right?"

I rubbed the back of my head again and looked up to see Mattie.

"I think so," I said slowly. "Just banged up a bit."

I tucked my hair behind my ear and realized my hand was bleeding.

Mattie took me by the arm and hauled me up, making me yelp, but I clutched Daisy close. I wasn't about to put her down now.

"Are you *sure* you're okay?"

I nodded. "Yeah. I just...it was so sudden, and I freaked out."

The door to the car finally opened and a young man stepped out. He couldn't be much past high school. He was pale from the accident, but he didn't look towards me. He had nearly killed me and Daisy, and he didn't even meet my eyes or try to apologize. Instead, he cursed and kicked his car as if it were somehow responsible for him speeding. I narrowed my eyes in fury, which was burning through me, lessening the pain.

I waited to see if he would turn, but if anything, he deliberately didn't. He slowly turned the other way in an act of pure, deliberate ignoring.

I stepped forward, nearly tripped, and shouted, "*What* is *wrong* with you?"

"Whoa, lady," he said, finally turning to hold up his hands. He backed up as if *I* were the one in the wrong.

"You could have killed me!" I shrieked, pushing my hair out of my face and seeing my bloody hands again. "You could have slaughtered my puppy!"

"Hey now," he said backing up further and looking around for support.

I glanced around too, checking to see if I was being totally irrational, but I didn't know these people and they were gawking silently. I *had* almost been killed. I had *every* right to be furious. How dare he act like I was the crazy one?

"What were you thinking?" I started towards him again, but Mattie grabbed my forearm. I yelped.

"Rosemary," Mattie said gently. "You better not."

"I am going to kick some sense into his stupid, reckless, harmful, damaging, irresponsible head," I swore. Then whimpered. "Ow."

"Calm down," Mattie said, jerking her head to the side as a cop car pulled to a stop. A moment later an ambulance arrived.

"I am..." I struggled to find a word for my fear and shock and finished lamely, "not very happy."

I looked at the cop as he approached. His face was calm. He was an older man with a gray mustache and an athlete's build.

"What happened here?"

"He could have killed me speeding through town like a fool."

"I heard," the cop said. "Are you all right?"

"No," I shouted, but not at the cop, at the kid. "No. I am not all right." My new boots were scuffed, my puppy was afraid, I was bruised, bleeding, and I *hurt.*

"She's bleeding on her hands. And her arm is messed up," Mattie told the cop.

"Get her on over to the ambulance. I'll take care of this," the cop said. He walked towards the kid like they'd done this before.

I went grumbling and found my new coat had a hole in it. Seeing that hole made my eyes tear up. My palms were bleeding and the blood had gotten onto my new sweater.

It wasn't only an EMT in the ambulance. There was a nurse and the doctor from the tiny, local clinic as though they didn't have enough business to stay behind. It made it easier though. I got a prescription for pain pills right there on the sidewalk and my hands and elbow wrapped up.

"This is weird," I told Dr. Jane. She was a few years older than me with black hair pulled back into a bun and no makeup. I liked her instantly because she was as mad about the accident as I was. She had spent most of the time wrapping me up muttering about idiot children who shouldn't be allowed to drive. She checked Daisy over, too.

"Isn't it?" she asked. Her face had been serious, but she flashed me a grin. "You were lucky. You have good reflexes and instincts."

"She's moving here, Janey," Mattie said. "She hasn't said what she's up to, but Simon already asked her out."

"Did he? Is she, Mattie? Wine night?"

"For sure," Mattie agreed. "She's definitely wine night material."

"What?" I had hit my head hard or they were good enough friends that they didn't need to speak so others could follow.

"For sure," Mattie repeated. "Tomorrow night. Not it."

"Not it."

They turned and looked at me in unison. Their heads tilted as one and together they said, "Her place."

"What?"

"Your place. Tomorrow. After work," Mattie said. "It'll be perfect."

"Wine, pizza, dessert." Dr. Jane looked at me as if I should have known.

"For sure," Mattie added. "Your place. Mine is a hovel that you can't see until after you love me. Hers has teenagers. Your place. Wine. Pizza. Dessert. *Gossip.*"

"Can I drink wine and have these?" I asked, waving my prescription. I hoped that was agreement enough. My head was pounding.

"It's a bad idea," Dr. Jane said. "But I won't stop you. No driving though. For now, you better take these."

She turned to the nurse who handed me ibuprofen and a muscle relaxer.

"This ambulance is crazy," I told her shaking my head. This would never have happened in Gresham or Portland.

"Welcome to Silver Falls." Jane winked. "If this pain doesn't get better in a couple of days, you come in and get an x-ray," she said. I blinked at the switch back from casual to professional.

I glanced at my phone. The screen was broken. My teeth ground in renewed fury.

Mattie followed my gaze. "Oh man. You'll have to go to Lincoln City to get a new one. Or wait until one gets delivered."

I glanced back at the kid. My eyes narrowed in sheer, unadulterated rage and my murdered phone had re-ignited the injustice of it all.

"I'll get one sent to me," I sighed. It was nearly seven, and I had a date. I downed the pills Dr. Jane gave me without water, brushed off my butt, and made sure I could walk without limping too bad. Mattie took my bloody sweater and gave me hers. It was a gray knee-length thing that worked for my outfit—not as well—but it was okay. And it wasn't bloody. I picked my coat off the ground from where I'd dropped it and held my arms out for inspection.

"Good enough," Mattie said.

"Good enough is good enough I guess," I said. "I gotta go."

I took a moment to pull down the sleeves on my sweater to cover the bandages and put my coat back on. I ran my fingers through my hair, and said, "Tomorrow. My place. Wine. Pizza. Dessert. Doc, you're gonna have to keep me alive because I'm drinking and probably taking those pills, too."

She grinned, and Mattie said, "See you."

I walked over to talk to the police officer, gavehim my version of events, and then left for my date.

I WALKED UP TO SIMON WITH MY HEART IN MY THROAT. DAISY WAS tripping beside me, charming every passing child, but his slow smile was what warmed me up and calmed me down after being so angry. Though, the muscle relaxers were probably helping too.

"Hello there," he said. He lifted a basket and held out his arm.

I had to pause to enjoy the sheer gentlemanliness of the gesture before I tucked my hand into the crook of his arm and let him lead the way to the blanket. He'd laid it down towards the side of the park, out of the line of foot traffic, and was surrounded by enough people who knew him that it was clearly a spot the locals knew to grab.

"This is fun," I said, dropping my elbow to settle onto the blanket and forcing my face to hide the pain of sitting on the ground. There was a graying black lab already laying on the blanket, and the puppy Simon adopted was tucked next to the older dog. His head lifted as

Daisy skipped over and they touched noses before Daisy dared to face the big dog. The old black lab was calm enough and mature enough to simply look at Daisy and lay his head back down.

Simon handed me a thermos cup from his bag. With the sleeves of Mattie's sweater hooked over my thumb, my bandages were hidden. The bag was one of those insulated grocery store bags, and I was pretty sure I smelled fried chicken.

"Did you name him?" I asked, grateful for something that eased us into conversation and out of awkwardness.

"Duke," he said.

I snorted and he looked up.

"You don't like Duke?"

I couldn't hold back a laugh. "Meet Daisy."

His laugh was a low chuckle and I enjoyed it immensely.

I took a grateful sip from the cup he'd given me and grinned even wider when I tasted the Irish cream in the coffee.

"Ooh," I said. "Lovely."

"I wasn't sure," he replied. "I have cocoa too if you'd prefer."

"This is perfect," I said, flashing back to the near-miss with the car and feeling grateful for something that would help me relax and maybe dull the coming aches. "You're a cop?"

"The only detective on the force in our small town."

"Oooh." I noticed the side-long glances from the people around us and wondered if this was what it was like to live in a small town. Were they looking at me only because of him? Or was it something about me that was catching their attention?

No, they were only taking note of their friend and neighbor. These people were talking amongst themselves like long-time friends, and they didn't blink twice at the people who were more likely tourists.

"How was your first day in Silver Falls?" Simon asked, ignoring the people around us.

"Um," I said, thinking for a second. "Mostly good. Very surreal. It's pretty weird to be starting a new life."

I didn't want to dwell on the near-miss. I'd rather focus on how lucky I'd been to get away with a few scratches and an unscathed puppy. I tucked my loose hair behind my ear. Even with Mattie's careful styling and products, my frizzy red hair had broken free from confinement. Or maybe that was just the accident. I didn't care. The moon started to rise and the music was as amazing as the food. Given my company and surroundings, the day ended up being almost perfect after all.

❦ 4 ❦

"Well, well, well," Zapphirah said as I walked into the diner. It had been a few weeks since I bought the diner and we'd started working together, but Zapphirah hadn't stopped given me constant sass. She was in her late sixties, and her white hair had been dyed a brilliant red and faded to pale pink with white roots, which looked awesome. She'd worked at the diner since it had opened and spent the entirety of everyday harassing every single person who came into the diner who knew her. She even gave the tourists a fair amount of cheekiness but was able to get away with it by coming off like a grandma. Given that the only reason she wasn't retired was she was too spiteful to spend her days relaxing, she worked exactly how she wanted and it didn't matter one bit that I owned the diner now. "Doesn't the new sign look *fancy*."

Zapphirah's tone said the new sign was comparable to a dead rat on the sidewalk. Her glance back at the new flooring and reupholstered booths said that she thought those might be on par with some sort of foot fungus.

"I think it looks nice," I said brightly, as if it wasn't the most beautiful thing I had *ever* seen. The words "2nd Chance Diner" were painted where "Jenny's" had once been.

I took off my coat and scarf and grinned as I looked around. The diner had been closed for three days during the week while new flooring had been installed and the booths had been recovered. The diner walls, which had been a pale green, were now a pretty soft grey with watercolors from local artists on the walls. The new curtains on the bay windows were all that I'd ever wanted for the diner.

I hadn't changed the layout, so people still came in to see a long display case of desserts behind the counter and stools, which let the lone diners stare at the baked goods while they ate. The counter ended where the dining area widened with twenty tables and booths and a backroom for parties.

"Looks real nice, Rose," Az, our cook, said from the other side of the order window. "Real, real nice."

"Doesn't it?" My voice was a squeak of excitement, and he grinned at the sound, which was all too alike a mouse on helium.

Az was a brilliant cook. He'd learned my recipes and adjusted them to make them even better. He was a huge man, at least 6'5, nearly as dark as night, with deep, kind, chocolate eyes, and the best set of dreadlocks I'd ever seen. Plus, he had a Jamaican accent that made me want to listen to him call 'Order up' all day long. To be perfectly honest though, I wasn't sure I'd ever hate anyone calling out 'Order Up' in my diner. Every time someone ate in my diner—especially with my recipes—it cemented that my dream had come to life.

I walked to the backroom, hung up my scarf and coat, told Daisy to lay down in her bed, and went into the kitchen with my apron on.

"I was thinking," I told Az, "we could do a competition next Sunday for the Spaghetti and Meatballs challenge, Jenny's classic versus my version. Have like a multi-course meal for a flat fee and make a party of it. Maybe free drinks, minus the alcohol, and specialized, extra expensive desserts."

I started prepping chicken fried steak while he moved so fast I wasn't sure I'd ever be able to match him. The first customers were coming through the door. It was only 6:00 a.m., and it was mostly locals who came for breakfast given that the high season had ended and the few tourists in Silver Falls tended to sleep in.

"I think this place is your thing, little love," Az said through his thick accent. "You wanna have a competition and compare recipes, you do it. Might be fun." He had an accent that sounded like rapids in the river, all rumbly and fantastic. He'd pulled his dreadlocks back into a ponytail while his beard was cut close to his chin. He was the favorite of my staff, and I hoped he'd never leave.

"You sure you want to call her 'little love,' Az?" Zapphirah called from the window. She slapped a ticket down. "Order in. She could be Satan's mistress. She might be planning to fire us all now that Jenny can't stop her."

"Or I could be awesome," I suggested, and Zapphirah snorted before she walked away in her beige orthotic shoes, light blue uniform dress, and her giant chunky jewelry.

"Now, don't mind Zee, luv," Az said. "She's all lemon juice and vinegar. She's not so bad under all that anger and meanness."

I grinned at him and then went to the front, Daisy tripping behind me the moment I left the kitchen. She settled in her bed near the hostess stand.

"Hello," I said as the doorbell rang and looked up to find Simon and Jane.

"Hello there," Simon said. His gaze roved over my face and body but lingered on my smile, which made him essentially intoxicating.

I was the boss, right? Right! I sat with Simon and Jane for breakfast and ignored Zee's sideways comments about it. Jane and Simon were cousins, but they acted more like brother and sister. I felt like I had the beginnings of a great set of friendships. I was letting things roll with Simon and I had to admit I very much liked how and where they were going. And I was still going to go to the knitting circle at the end of the month let alone having my wine night.

Zee passed our table, filled Simon's coffee cup without a word, then snapped at the man the next booth over. "That's enough Coke for you, Leroy. You're hanging over the top of your jeans again."

"Zee, you old cow," Leroy replied mildly. "That's no way to get a tip."

"Your wife finds out you stiff me, Leroy Parker, and you'll hear about it later. Especially for looking after you. You think she wants you to keel over dead?" Zee considered for a moment. "Well, maybe she does. I'm sure you don't appreciate her."

"Now, Zee," Leroy said, dropping cash on the table, "don't be like that."

A few moments later, our second waitress came through the door. Tara was young and late every day, but everyone loved her and she worked hard once she finally showed up.

"You're late, Tara," Zee snarled as she took down a plate. She set it in front of a man at the bar and filled coffee cups down the line of the bar.

"Sorry, Zee," Tara yelped and ran to the back.

I grinned at Simon as Jane put her cash on the table. She stopped long enough to say, "Have a good one. Are you doing the spaghetti thing?"

I nodded. Jane winked and left, adjusting her coat over her scrubs.

Simon leaned back, took a slow sip of his coffee, and set his cup back down. I had to grin at the sheer laziness of his movements. Every once in a while, he reminded me of his old dog that snuggled into every spot, lolled about, and lived for lengthy stretches. I didn't get his life. Was Silver Falls so lacking in single women that he was alone? He seemed far more handsome than someone with my thickish behind, frizzy red hair, and the new zit on my chin could interest. I liked myself well enough, but for too long no one else had seen anything about me to like. Why did he?

Nope, Rose, I thought—enough of that. I was awesome. I'd just been looking for someone who recognized how great I was. I wasn't sure I found that in Simon, but I wasn't going to pretend that he wasn't somehow out of my class. Frizzy hair or not.

"You doing okay with Zee?" He glanced towards where the sour woman was flashing a rare bit of sweetness as she talked to a young mom and her two little kids.

"I'm not worried about Zee," I said. I grinned, looked over my shoulder to ensure that Zee couldn't hear me. "She's delightfully spicy."

Simon leaned forward, with his gaze on my lips. "I'm glad you think so."

He didn't kiss me, but I was pretty sure he'd been thinking about it.

"Sunday? Spaghetti and meatballs? Blind taste test?"

"Absolutely," he said.

My grin couldn't be kept back, so I cleared the table to feel a little less awkward about how excited I was.

☙❦❧

"TARA," I SAID ON SUNDAY AS SHE LEFT FOR HER BREAK BEFORE THE spaghetti event. "Be on time for the event, please."

"Sure, Rose," Tara said as she ran out the door. She hadn't been on time yet, but I reminded myself that I liked her. Az told me she'd broken up with her boyfriend, but given that she'd been unreliable since she was hired—according to Zee—I didn't think that was much of an excuse. I suspected that she was one of those people who thought you could do more in ten minutes than was possible.

"She's never going to be on time," Zee snapped. "I suppose you'll fire her even though she's a dumb kid."

"Daisy likes her," I said to Zee mildly. "I think we'll keep her around."

"I've been on the clock all day," Zee snapped. "I'm sitting down with my girls and having some pasta. And don't think I'll be here in the morning. Cause I won't. We haven't been open on Mondays in all my days here and that's my day off."

"I hope you have a good time with your friends. Monday is still our day off," I assured her as the first of our customers came in for the event.

Weclosed at 2:00 pm and opened again at 4:30 pm, but we'd all stayed behind to help in the kitchen. I had no idea how many meatballs to make, but I didn't want to run out. Az assured me we'd be fine, but I wasn't taking any chances. I'd rather have way too many and serve them in weird ways in the coming days or give them to the local pet shelter instead of having too few.

The 2nd Chance Diner filled up faster than I expected. I didn't think free iced tea, coffee, or soda would have been that much of a draw. And yet my tables were all full. Even with the free drinks, I could see the money inside my head. We were well on our way to having the best revenue day since my purchase of 2nd Chance.

"Hello there," I said as the bell rang again without even looking up.

"Rose!" Mattie shouted, and I turned towards her. She was glancing around, taking in the people waiting for tables, and giving me a thumbs up. "It smells amazing in here."

"Yeah, it does," Simon said. He'd walked in without me noticing Jane was behind him. Seeing my friends on my big night made everything better.

"I hope you're hungry," I told them. My hands were shaking, so I handed them the specialty menus I'd had printed up in an effort to hide my nerves. There were so many people, and the food was going so fast. Az had pulled in his brother to help him make even more meatballs and another huge pot of sauce.

I should have been helping in the kitchen, but I was spending so much time clearing tables, seating people, and refilling drinks I hadn't been able to do more than ask Az what he needed, try to grab things from the fridge and bring them back. If we'd had a full menu instead of the choice between vegetarian and spaghetti with meatballs, we'd have been in trouble.

"I'll be back," I said, running to clear the table in the corner. It was near the restrooms and a side door to the kitchen, and pretty much the worst table in the house, but I was going to seat my friends early. I'd feel less bad about it if I gave them the worst table.

"You're doing great," Simon said, sliding his arm around my shoulders and giving me a sideways hug. Jane and Mattie noticed. As did Zee with her razor-sharp eyes and...once I thought about it...half the town.

Even still, I let the heat of him sink into me and borrowed the confidence in his voice. I needed those things, and I reminded myself that I was going to *own* my second chance. I led them to the table, hoping that I'd be able to take a break with them.

It didn't happen. We were *flooded* with people. Tara was late. Of course she was, but it irritated Zee, who'd finished eating and scowled at the people waiting for food and drinks. Zee got up to deliver plates, cursing the whole time, and then chewed out Tara when she arrived.

"Zee," I said. "You're making it worse."

Given that Tara was near tears, I told her, "It's all right. Go take a deep breath. It's only spaghetti."

"It's your big night," Tara said as she sniffed. She wiped her face with shaking hands. "I just...things have been...I'm sorry..."

"Maybe you could take out Daisy for me?" I asked to give her time to gather her emotions. "It's been too long. And then maybe crate her in the back? I think it's a bit too busy in here for her."

Daisy was fine, but I needed Tara to be capable of working.

I took the next round of plates out and when I got back, Tara was pale but steady. Zee had kept serving, and the rhythm of our normal days was coming back even though everything was different for Spaghetti night. It was impossible to tell if Zee was having fun chatting with everyone or if she was furious about working, but she'd gotten up of her own volition and I was willing to take her help.

"This," Mattie said when I stopped by her friends' table, "is a raving success."

"Which meatballs do you like better?"

Each plate was served with four meatballs with two that had red toothpicks and two that had blue toothpicks.

"Red," Mattie said as Jane said, "Blue."

The three women turned to Simon, who said, "Rose's are the red ones, and they're amazing."

"That doesn't answer the question," I said laughing.

He grinned and shrugged. "We'll see what the people say."

I gasped and turned to the others. "He prefers Jenny's."

"He's a man who doesn't like change," Jane said. "Never did. Pancakes on Mondays. Scrambled eggs on Tuesdays."

"Shut it," Simon said mildly to Jane, who was laughing too hard to continue.

"I prefer eggs over medium on a bagel on Tuesdays," I said. "Clearly there is something wrong with him. Scrambled eggs are all wrong for Tuesdays."

"Clearly," Mattie said. "Someone else is going to snatch up Rose and her food-making-ways while Simon dillydallies and struggles over the *better* meatballs."

Simon tangled his fingers with mine and said, "We'll see."

"I am not something to be snatched," I told Mattie virtuously. "Though I am, of course, a prize beyond measure. Back to spaghetti," I said, winking and teasing so naturally I forgot we'd only been friends for a few weeks.

I moved back to refill glasses and stopped in my tracks. The first table had the *jerk* who'd nearly run me and Daisy down. I thought for a moment about kicking him out of my restaurant but decided not to. Instead, I walked over and asked, "Pepsi?"

He looked up and nodded but his gaze wasn't focusing on me. He slowly blinked. I noticed the sweat on his face. Was he high? Or sick?

"Are you all right?"

His head bopped towards me and then he fell out of the booth and onto the floor.

"Kyle!" The girl across from him shouted and threw herself down on the floor next to him. The buzz of happy noise in the restaurant faded as people heard the girl calling his name.

"Jane!" I shouted. "Jane!"

I turned to get the doctor, but she was already running across the restaurant, Simon behind her.

"What happened?" Simon asked.

"I...I don't know," I replied. "He was acting funny. I asked him if he was okay, and he just fell..."

"Call for the ambulance, Simon," Jane said. "Quick."

"Is it food poisoning?" a customer asked, sounding panicked.

That thought struck me cold, and I shook my head frantically, looking at the customer's doubtful face. Goodness no. We were careful. We abided by all the food safety laws.

Zee said, "Of course it isn't, you fool. There'd be more than one person sick. He probably overdosed. Like we don't know he's a drug addict."

"He didn't," the girl on the ground next to him said. She wiped her tears away and whimpered, "Kyle...he wouldn't."

Zee scoffed down at the girl. "Kyle Johansson is trouble," she said snidely. "I've seen him high more than once."

"He said he stopped," the girl said. She wiped her tears away and repeated, "He said he stopped."

"What does he use?" Jane demanded, glancing at the girl from where she was working on the kid. "Tell me."

"I don't know. I don't do that stuff." The girl was openly crying now, tears rolling down her face. She wasn't a loud crier—more of a little sniffle here and there with a stream of tears.

"You know what he uses, Morgan," Simon said and then ordered, "Tell us the truth."

"He uses pot," Tara said. I looked over, not even realizing she had been there. "Sometimes some ecstasy. Whatever is easy to get. Oxy a few times. If he could steal it from someone."

"He doesn't do it anymore," Morgan shouted, still wiping her tears away. "He wouldn't. *I* don't like it. He wouldn't. He promised."

The 'wouldn't' was a cracked plea, and I was pretty sure that the poor girl didn't believe herself. I certainly didn't, and if the expression on Jane's face was any indication, she didn't believe it either.

Simon moved people back and we stopped serving food until Kyle was moved out of the restaurant. Tara burst into tears and ran towards the office with Zee following. The look on her face was one of concern, and I was surprised to see real affection behind the usual anger, and the only thing coming out of her mouth was soft little tut-tuts.

I looked to Az for an explanation. "Tara and Kyle have dated off and on since kindergarten."

"Oh man." I'd had no idea that guy was Tara's ex. What a *jerk* to come to this restaurant with someone else.

"Morgan was her friend," Az muttered. "Supposedly."

"Do we keep serving?"

"We can't do anything about Kyle," Az said. "Zee is right. That kid was bad news. And this was an overdose."

"Turn the music up a bit," Mattie said. She grabbed a plate and started serving, laughing off bringing the food to the wrong places, but Az coached her as he handed her plates, and we took up a new rhythm. I refilled drinks and handed out cookies and did whatever I could to enliven the place. With the shock fading, some of the fun returned, subdued though it was.

5

"What even happened?" I asked at the end of the night. The rest of the evening had been subdued. I think that all of us who'd been there when Kyle collapsed were worried about his chances. Jane's face had been tight with worry, and given that she'd been a doctor, I took that pretty seriously. That kid...that stupid, moronic kid might be dying.

We kept moving and serving because what else were we supposed to do? The restaurant stayed busy and after the customers who'd witnessed Kyle's collapse left, 2nd Chance upped in energy. It wasn't as cheery as before because rumors were flying. Tara disappeared to cry in the back, and Az and his brother, Eddie, spent as much time talking to her as shouting, "Order up."

"This was lovely fun," Paige from the little boutique nearby said. She squeezed my shoulder. "I'm sorry to hear about the boy. You did what you could, sugar."

"Everyone is so nice," I told my crew as Paige left. We'd stopped seating a while ago and Az had used the time to clean the kitchen, so we were able to leave as soon as the dessert cabinet and tables were wiped down and the floor was mopped.

Tara nodded, sniffing, and Az wrapped an arm around her yet again.

"There, there lamb," he said. "It'll be all right. You want some company? Eddie and I have a nice guest bedroom. No need to be alone."

"He's going to die," Tara said, the tears starting again. "He's going to die and we were so angry at each other. I'll never speak to him again, and I didn't get to tell him all he needed to know."

"There, there," Az crooned again. He squeezed her against him. "It's in God's hands, kitten. Don't worry. Those are good hands to be in."

Tara wailed before she tucked her head into Az's shoulder.

Zee, however, snorted. "This isn't God. This is what comes from poor parenting."

"Oh, Zee," I protested, but she carried on without a pause.

"Poor parenting, a lack of a moral compass, and entitled children who have never been taught to respect their elders."

Az ignored Zee, but Mattie looked the woman over. "How does lack of respect for you end up with a kid overdosing on drugs?"

Zapphirah put a hand to her chest as if she'd been personally attacked. "A lack of social consciousness..."

"Oh, Zee," I said again, but in a different tone.

Her gaze shot to me with full daggers out.

"Thank you so much for your help tonight," I continued. "You too, Mattie. And your brother, Az, I'll figure out payment and..."

"No money," Mattie interjected. "Wine. And cake and your hot tub. Please?"

I nodded instantly. That was an excellent deal since I knew she'd share.

Az nodded and jerked his head at Eddie towards the back.

"Enjoy your day off tomorrow," I told the others and gave Tara a quick hug, "Don't give up hope, Tara. Medicine can do amazing things."

She sniffed and gave me a watery smile before darting out the door. I could hear a loud sob, but she was gone in a few steps, and finally, the sound of crying faded. Zee followed after her. She hesitated and turned back as she said, "Your meatballs were good, girl. I haven't had tips this good in a long time. Given the look of you, I'd have expected Jenny's Diner to fail by now."

"Ouch," Az said for me. He took his share of the tips and nodded to everyone fading into the darkness.

I didn't see the point in responding to Zee's venom. "Have a good night."

I'd walked to 2nd Chance and my feet were aching. Mattie glanced around and then walked to the wine cabinet and dug through. She put one bottle in her bag, glanced at me and went back for a second.

I boxed the last of the chocolate cake for us as Mattie's phone buzzed.

"Jane is coming. She says to get her cake too. And leftovers. And bread."

I yawned, considered, and yawned again.

"I never want spaghetti again," I told Mattie as we walked out the door. I whistled for Daisy, remembered that I'd had her crated, and ran back for her.

"Did you tally the votes?" Mattie asked. "Because I think people would come back for this. You should do it every Sunday night."

"Themed nights?"

"Yes. Themed nights. Limited menu. Free drinks. Make it a tradition and see if you can't get people to come regularly."

By the time we'd reached the house, the adrenaline of the evening had faded and my feet were pulsating with pain. I put on my swimsuit and sank into the hot tub with a sigh.

"My feet hurt so bad," I told Mattie. She nodded and handed me a glass of wine. She beat me to the hot tub, but I had to run a brush over Daisy, feed her, and move her bed next to the window so she could see us.

"I'd say I don't know why you want to have a diner given my current pain," Mattie said as she rubbed her feet, "but I suppose I'm on my feet all day too."

I laid back in the water until I was almost entirely submerged except for my ears and my face.

"Do you think the kid will live?" I asked as I sat up.

Mattie shook her head. "Jane said it didn't look good. He was flown to Seaside Hospital. He's fallen into a coma. She doesn't expect him to come out of it."

"Oh man," I hadn't liked that kid. Not one bit after he'd nearly killed me and Daisy and hadn't apologized or even seemed distressed, but he was young. He might have matured. Become less deadly to mankind in general. "So, he and Tara dated?"

"Yeah," Mattie stretched out her neck, took a sip of her wine, and said, "They were the couple that needed to be separated but never quite got rid of the other. Tara's sweet until she's around Kyle. Then she's sort of territorial and crazy. We all hoped after the last breakup that they'd stay broken up. Tara's a good kid, y'know?"

"I like her," I said, and I did. She was tardy all the time, but she was bright and happy when she worked, and she worked hard. She didn't have a problem delivering Zee's food or scrubbing the grill for Az or taking Daisy out for me. "I hope she'll be okay."

The doorbell rang, and Mattie and I looked at each other. Mattie shouted to come in and a moment later, Jane walked in.

"You made good time," I said. It had been hours, but the drive from Seaside to Silver Falls wasn't short. "Why Seaside Hospital?"

"Given the nature of what was happening." Jane said. "The hospital in Seaside was a better choice, but I left as soon as I handed him off."

"Will he make it?"

Jane hesitated. "Maybe. He's young."

She made a face and my heart hiccupped. I didn't want to think of that stupid, dumb kid dead. I wanted to think of him picking up trash on the side of the freeway for being a jerk driver.

Jane continued, admitting, "I doubt it. Nothing we're doing is helping. He's not responding to the drug overdose meds. I got a message about him from the doctor at the hospital, but I just can't check it. Is he dead? I can't look yet. I want to drink some wine and let it go for now."

Mattie pointed to the bottle of wine, and Jane joined us a moment later.

"So, has Simon kissed you yet?" Jane asked.

I dunked my head under the water to hide the blush. No. He hadn't. Why? It was probably the frizzy hair.

When I came up for air, Jane said dryly, "I'll take that as a no."

"What does Simon say about Rose?" Mattie sipped her wine, but her expression was wicked. I suppose I couldn't blame her since I was all ears.

Jane glanced at me, then at Mattie. "Oh, you know...she's a nice girl. Nothing, really. He's not stupid. He's noticed our wine nights."

"It's unfortunate that he's so observant," Mattie said. "My life and your life are worthless for gossip."

"Not true," said Jane. "You just have to be interested in the drama of the 8th grade."

"Pass," Mattie said, and I nodded. Even if Mattie cared, which she assuredly didn't, I didn't even know the kids or their families. Gossip about people you didn't know was no fun.

"Listen—" I began, but there was a knock on the door. The three of us looked at each other before standing together. I put on my robe, followed by Jane and Mattie. Daisy wasn't barking, which made me wonder if it was Simon, but showing up like this was not like him.

I toed Daisy to the side from where she was sitting at the door, tail wagging, and peeked through the peephole.

"Who is it?" Mattie asked. She didn't sound concerned, but I knew she was. It had been on her face when we'd heard the knock.

"It's Simon," I said as I opened the door. "Hey."

He didn't smile at me like he normally did, and he glanced over at Mattie and Jane. "Good. You're all here. How drunk are you?"

"Not at all," I said. I hadn't been drunk since my early twenties.

"Good," he said again. He rubbed Daisy's ears, but I suspected it was out of habit because there was no light in his eyes.

"What's going on?"

"It wasn't an overdose," Simon told Jane. "It was insulin poisoning."

Jane's face dropped into shock horror. "I...we...we might have been able to help more if we weren't treating drugs."

"Is he diabetic?" I asked. I took a sip of my wine before setting the glass on the countertop to start a pot of coffee. It was too late for coffee, but I suspected we wouldn't be sleeping anytime soon with or without coffee.

"You couldn't have known, Jane. There wasn't any reason to suspect insulin." Mattie had taken hold of Jane's arm.

"Especially with the history of drugs, right?"

Jane's face said she didn't agree, but Simon didn't wait to comfort Jane.

"He didn't have access to insulin," Simon said. "His mom was very clear."

I sat down. "What are you saying?"

"It's attempted murder, Rose," he said. "Someone tried killed Kyle Johannson."

6

"**W**ho served his table?" Simon asked.

I stared at him. My mind tripped over itself as I realized what he was asking.

He was asking who had tried to kill Kyle. In *my* diner. In *my* 2nd Chance. This was *not* happening.

I shook my head and then asked, with a plea in my voice, "Why are you so sure this isn't self-inflicted?"

"We have to assume it isn't until we prove otherwise," Simon said. His face had aged since I'd seen him last.

This was *not* okay. None of this was okay. That first booth in my diner had been a place where a person had almost *died*. Who still might die. When it had been an overdose, it had upset me. It had taken a bit of the gloss off my 2nd Chance. But this was so much worse. Someone deliberately trying to take the kid's life away, before he'd even had a chance to ruin his first chance and then have a second one.

"I...no..." No. No.

"I'm sorry, Rose," Simon said. He didn't take my hand though. And his face stayed firm. There was nothing that was soft or interested in his gaze now.

"Oh my..." I stared at him, feeling a rising sense of horror. "I'm a suspect."

His face blanked as Mattie cursed and Jane said, "Simon..."

"Anyone who handled the food is suspect. Until we know more."

"Well," I said, trying to sound confident, "if I'm going to be interviewed about attempted murder, I'd like to have some clothes on."

I left the living room. My hands were shaking as I toweled my hair dry, took off my suit and put on some jeans and a cozy sweater. I definitely needed a cozy hug of a sweater to be interviewed as a murder suspect.

I walked back to the living room and poured myself a mug of coffee. Daisy was leaning against Simon's leg, the traitor.

I handed a mug each to Jane and Mattie without asking them if they wanted one. It took a moment for me to be willing to give Simon a cup too, but I did. I was just so *mad* at being a suspect.

"It was a mess," I told him as I grudgingly shoved him a cup of coffee. He was a trained investigator, so I was sure he saw how angry I was and how little I wanted to give him coffee. "We were *all* serving each other's tables. And the food was all the same. You saw. The only options were spaghetti with meatballs or without for the vegetarians. Anyone could have served that food."

"Whose table was it?"

I shook my head. "It isn't that easy. With Zee—she does what needs to be done, so we all sort of help each other out and pool the tips. Everyone works together to keep the customers happy. Even on a normal day, anyone could have helped at that table."

"But whose table was it?" His voice was steady, but it *irritated* me how much he wasn't listening. It was Tara's, but I was pretty sure I'd delivered the spaghetti. Or maybe I'd refilled the drinks. And, of course, nearly every plate had gone through Az's hands. Zee walked the entire diner making sure that people had bread and refilled drinks.

"It was Tara's," I finally said when the weight of his gaze wouldn't let me avoid it anymore.

"And Tara and Kyle used to date?" Simon asked me.

"They haven't dated since I've known Tara. That's all I can tell you." I snapped.

As if I hadn't been well aware that Tara was broken up over her boyfriend. I liked Tara. And it could have been anyone who poisoned that kid. This was so wrong. It was all so wrong. Tara and Zee and Az, they were becoming my family.

Simon sighed, and I felt a tiny bit guilty before the anger came back.

"You saw the restaurant," I told him. "It was packed. What is insulin even like? Girls get roofied all the time in bars with their drinks nearby. It isn't the staff who is the first suspect. A distraction at the right time and anyone could have done it. Anyone could have tried to kill that kid. Or am I supposed to have randomly selected someone to kill?" I was rambling, spilling out every idea that came to me, but I didn't care.

"Rose," Mattie squeaked and then dramatically shut her mouth.

"He's doing his job," Jane said gently. "No one here thinks you did it. Why would you?"

I met Simon's eyes, and I could see that he could think of a few reasons. I didn't know how seriously he took those reasons, but I was pretty sure that they were clunking around in his head. I'd read enough murder mysteries to come up with a few without too much trouble. I wasn't sure what this would do to our friendship after he realized that *of course* I didn't want to kill that poor kid.

"I know," I said grudgingly. "It doesn't make me love being a suspect, either."

"It's okay, Rose," Mattie said.

"It'll be fine," Jane replied. "Simon is very good at what he does."

I couldn't forget the fact that I was new here. Jane and Mattie and Simon had gone to grade school together, grown up, and then come back to continue their friendships. This town was full of those people. *I* was the outsider, and as the newest of the outsiders, surely I was the most disposable? I was playing with things like the beloved 'Jenny's Meatballs,' and maybe my fairytale happily-ever-after in my 2nd Chance was going to crumble into dust.

What if they didn't find who'd actually poisoned Kyle but they couldn't prove it wasn't me? Would I be a suspect forever? Would I be selling 2nd Chance Diner and hoping for a way to a third chance? How many chances did I need before I would give up and go back to Gresham?

"Just tell me what you remember," Simon said.

"I...I went over and asked Kyle if he wanted a refill. I..." I didn't want to say it, but I figured that the best route would be to be entirely honest. "I recognized him. I hadn't seen him in the diner before, but after the accident, I couldn't forget his face."

"You're holding a grudge?" Simon's voice was even.

"Simon!" Mattie protested as Jane whispered, "Hush. He has to ask."

My eye twitched. It was like I was on the phone again in the call center and someone was yelling at me about policies that I couldn't change.

I took a deep breath like I had done then. "Yeah. I was mad. Really mad. If I hadn't been paying attention—and I'd spent the entire day daydreaming—I could have died. Daisy could have died. I could have been crippled forever, and that punk didn't even apologize. He didn't care."

"You don't know that," Simon said in that same even, commanding voice. His eyes were fixed on my face, but there was no light in them like there had been before, and the change was too obvious to not see it.

I knew that voice. It was the one I'd used on the phones. Who would have even expected such a thing? Confident, calm, controlled. The same for call center reps as it was for police officers.

"I know he didn't apologize," I said in my controlled, calm, call-center voice. "It's not a motive. Not a real one."

Simon noticed the change in my tone. It wasn't one I had used since I quit my job, so none of my new friends had heard it, but it came back like an old friend. Or maybe like a wart you couldn't shake.

"Did you bring the food to the table?"

I took a deep breath. "I can't be sure, but I don't think so. Maybe."

"What about Tara? Do you know if Tara did?"

"It could have easily been either Tara or Zee. It was crazy in there. What if he went to the bathroom and left his plate unattended?" I lost my calm tone. "What if he had a drink before he came into 2nd

Chance? What if a hundred things? You can't prove it was my diner. That kid could have gotten that insulin stuff anywhere. You don't even know yet if he didn't do it to himself."

Simon didn't respond to any of that. Instead, he calmly asked, "Did Az ever say anything about Kyle?"

"No one ever talked about Kyle."

"Not even Tara?"

"Tara is a waitress who comes in late every day, leaves the second she is off and works hard while she is there. She is significantly younger than me, and I'm her new boss. She doesn't tell me *anything*. She cozies up and gives me crap lies to seek out the good shifts."

Simon glanced at me and then wrote down a note on his pad.

"Of course, she doesn't tell you anything," Mattie said consolingly. "I wouldn't either if I had a brand-new boss."

"Shhh," Jane hushed. "Mattie, shhhh."

Simon waited, so I carried on. "I don't know anything about her other than she eats a half a bagel with cream cheese and one slice of bacon for breakfast when she works in the mornings."

I took a sip of my coffee. It had gone cold, but I drank it anyway. I reminded myself that these people were not my enemies and that Simon was doing his job and that Mattie and Jane hadn't turned on me.

"I didn't poison that kid," I said. "I wouldn't even know how."

"No one is saying that, Rose," Mattie said.

"Anyone could Google how. Anyone with a diabetic in their lives. Are you diabetic, Rose?" Simon's voice had that same cool quality, but his gaze shifted that time.

I warmed at the sight of him not enjoying his job. It *was* his job.

Mattie took my hand and I let her. She squeezed and I squeezed back, grateful for the support.

It took me a moment to admit, "I'm freaking out. Someone attempted to murder...maybe...in my diner. And it's my second chance, it's my dream. I would have said that I hated that kid up until he started dying in front of me. I don't know why I love feeding people and seeing them find joy in their food, but I do, and this tarnishes it." My eyes burned with tears but I held them back.

"It's possible that it was self-inflicted. People do choose that way to die." Jane rose and took my cold coffee, dumped it in the sink and refilled it. "But Kyle wasn't diabetic. No one in his family was."

"How do you know that?" I asked, taking the warm cup of coffee and letting it heat my hands.

"Silver Falls isn't that big," Jane said. "I'm nearly everyone's doctor. Kyle's family is healthy like goats. They eat anything, they drink anything, and they're still sour cusses. The only thing that kills them is emphysema when they're so old they'd rather die anyway."

"But you're not Rose's doctor," Simon said.

"I *am* a doctor," Jane countered. "She's not diabetic. She doesn't have any signs of diabetes."

I rubbed my brow. "I'm not diabetic. My mom is not diabetic. The rest of my family are dead. My grandparents died in a car accident, my dad isn't around. I don't have siblings. I don't have close friends, but you know that."

Simon nodded and wrote another note.

"We don't know where the insulin came from," he said. "I can't be easy on you because I like you, Rose. I have to investigate this like any other crime. This was attempted murder. I shouldn't even be explaining myself now."

I nodded once, but I didn't have to like it. Any more than I liked how Daisy was leaning against his leg rather than mine or how his defection hurt more than a friendship of a couple of weeks should.

"Simon will find the killer," Mattie said. She was so soothing in her surety. As if I could count on him like she would be able to. I didn't know if that was true. I wanted it to be true. I wanted to believe that I'd found something special here, but it was all too new to believe.

7

I don't remember when I fell asleep, but when I woke, Jane was handing me a cup of coffee, and I realized I'd slept in one of the oversized chairs that faced the ocean. Daisy was curled up on my lap, and I was all too aware that I was no longer twenty-four years old.

I stretched, then whimpered.

"Oh man." Mattie sat up. "I should not have drunk the last of that wine or slept in my swim suit. What time is it?"

"Six," Jane said. She was eating a piece of toast and the moment she started to munch, Daisy abandoned me.

"Why am I awake?" Mattie moaned.

I sat up. The entire evening came back to me. "I can't live like this."

"Like what."

"Like a murder suspect."

Jane glanced at Mattie. "What do you plan to do about it?"

"I'm going to find out what happened."

"That's Simon's job," Mattie reminded me gently. "You can't interfere."

"I don't care. The main suspects are my staff. Maybe the girl that was with Kyle. And, of course, every other person that was in the restaurant." My voice was full of sarcasm, but I didn't even care. "Any-body who might have been with them outside. And the stupid kid."

I walked into my bedroom, took a shower, and when I came back, Jane was gone.

Mattie was drinking a cup of coffee, but she looked up. "Jane had to get to the office. They open early."

I nodded and crossed to my fridge. I didn't want to eat, but I knew if I didn't my body would betray me. I pulled out the blender and decided to make one of those green smoothies Jane praised me for. It wasn't like I had them every day. I didn't. I had them a few days a week. I ate pancakes at least once a week and had BLTs far more often than I should. I wasn't a saint, but I wasn't diabetic.

I made the green smoothie and slapped it on the table in front of Mattie.

"I want pancakes," she said, making a sad face.

"We'll get diabetes. Jane will give us insulin and then not stick up for us, and we'll get arrested," I told Mattie. "You were there too. You could have poisoned the kid."

"I have to work," she told me. She hesitated. "And Simon is mean when he gets angry. He'll get angry if we interfere. I'm not doing that. He holds grudges."

"I don't care," I said. "You guys aren't my only friends. Az is my friend, and he touched every plate that got served. Tara and Zee...well..."

Mattie's brows rose.

"Zee is like that crazy aunt that makes your teeth hurt but you love anyway. Tara is the stupid cousin you keep trying to help."

Mattie laughed at that. "I have an aunt like that." She hesitated before admitting, "And a cousin."

I HAD TO GO INTO THE DINER TO GET EVERYONE'S ADDRESSES. I sipped a fresh cup of coffee while I went and for once, drove my car. It had been quite a while since I'd driven it, but it started up with a purr, and I couldn't help but enjoy the fact that it was mine. My mom had been right that I needed a new car—I'd been driving the same ancient Honda Hatchback for more than a decade. As we drove, I scratched Daisy's ears which made her tail thump against the back of the front seat .

I pulled into the space in front of the diner. It was Monday and winter, so the town had only a few cars parked along Main Street in front of the tourist shops—most of which weren't open. I got out of the car and heard a crunch under my foot. I glanced down and found that I was standing in a paper bag from my diner that we used for left-overs and take-outs.

"People," I muttered, "are littering jerks."

I picked up the trash and whistled for Daisy. As I stepped onto the sidewalk, I found a sandwich wrapper that still had Jenny's printed on it. I frowned and picked that up too. As I straightened, I could see into the alleyway and found trash bags had been pulled out of the dumpster and ripped open, sending litter blowing onto the sidewalk.

This was not something that I'd seen happen in Silver Falls, and even though I was new, I was pretty sure this wasn't something that happened ever. Especially given that tourists were scarce this time of the year. Who would do this? We weren't a boutique that might be tossing anything worth dumpster-diving for. We threw away old food and paper products. Had someone been hungry?

I shook my head. After all that had happened, I wasn't sure this could be ignored. With a sigh, I pulled out my phone and called Simon.

"Rose?" His voice had none of the friendliness I'd been accustomed to. The switch was more painful than I wanted it to be.

"Someone dug through 2nd Chance's trash. Was it the police?"

He hesitated. "We did look through the trash, but how would you know?"

"It's everywhere," I snapped. "Did you really leave the diner like this? It's so rude."

I was done being patient and kind—not that I had been but *damn* it. Damn it!

"Of course, we didn't."

That gave me a much deeper, secondary chill.

"Well, someone did," I said. I sighed. "Did you want me to leave anything for you to look at or can I clean it up?"

I could hear Simon cover the phone and heard murmuring in the background.

"Leave it be," he said. "I'm sending Aaron Welsh over. He'll take a look around for extra evidence."

"Of course, if it was me or any of the staff," I said, sourly, "the evidence will be worthless given we are the ones who touched all of this originally. Or can you date fingerprints?"

I could hear him sigh. "Just leave it please, Rose. I'll be in touch."

He didn't wait for a goodbye, but I didn't have anything nice to say at that point anyway. I glanced around and then went into the diner to grab garbage bags. I wasn't going to leave the trash pouring around the street. I told Daisy to lay down in the office and went out with plastic gloves to pick up the trash in front of the street and on the sidewalk.

I had the bag half full when Paige from the little dress boutique opened her shop.

"You all right, sugar?"

"Some prankster messed around in the trash behind 2nd Chance," I said, standing up to stretch my back.

"Oh no." Paige glanced down her alleyway where her dumpster was and admitted, "I'm glad it didn't happen here."

"Yeah," I said. "It would have been awful if this had happened to everyone."

"You sure haven't been having very good luck the last few days. Poor Kyle overdosing and now this."

I blinked, surprised that gossip hadn't made the rounds and wondered who knew what had happened yet. As far as I knew, this was still an attempt at killing Kyle, and Jane hadn't seemed very hopeful about his survival. When the best that could be said was that you were young and your family was hearty, his chances didn't seem very promising.

"Hopefully things will improve," I said. "Did you know Kyle well?"

"Oh sure, since he was a kid. He was quite the handful, you know. I had hoped he and Tara would stay broken up this time. They never did. Not for long. Tara sure took it hard, but it would have been better for everyone. Those two are toxic together."

"Who was that girl who was with him?" I asked, grabbing another piece of trash and then letting the ocean breeze take away some of my concern. I felt *horrible,* of course. Being a murder suspect would do that to you. Except, I was also living my dream. That diner was *my* diner. This trash belonged to *my* dream. Even with all the bad, it was good.

"Morgan Brown."

"Are they dating?" I asked Paige. She seemed pretty tapped into the local gossip. I'd certainly been grilled the moment I bought the 2nd Chance Diner and started setting up.

"Oh, I don't think so," Paige replied. "She's like Tara and Kyle. Something of a, well, you don't want to say loser." Paige coughed delicately. "But that might be the most accurate term."

"Tara seems like a good kid to me," I said as I grabbed another piece of trash. I didn't want to offend Paige, but I did feel protective of my staff. "She works hard."

"Always late, I bet. I'm not sure that kid ever learned how to tell time."

"A few minutes, yeah," I hedged, not wanting to admit she'd *never* been on time. Not once.

"Mmm," Paige said, not believing me for a second. "Morgan is friends with Tara and Kyle. Always seemed like the third wheel to me. Even when they were kids poking starfish with sticks."

"That doesn't sound that great," I admitted. I couldn't imagine a young Tara poking starfish. Was I being naive? I wasn't sure.

"So they grew up together? The three of them?"

"Yeah. Morgan and Tara have been hooked at the hip since toddler days. When Tara and Kyle started dating, Morgan was just there too."

"Huh."

I saw the cop car pull up behind my Forrester. The cop walked towards the trash in the alley, and I didn't bother going over to say hello. Paige might not know I was suspected of trying to kill that stupid kid, but the cop would.

"Tara and Kyle breakup, and then Morgan tries to get them back together. It's very soap opera-y. Especially since Morgan seems to have decided to date him herself this time." Paige sighed. "Well...gotta go."

A person had walked into Paige's, and she went darting in after her customer. I stared after Paige, biting my lip as I thought about poor Tara and the drama of her life.

I glanced around to make sure I'd gotten all the trash that had blown out of the alley and then headed back toward the diner.

The cop looked up and glanced at me.

"Detective Banks said that you should leave the trash alone."

"I got the trash off the street. I haven't been in the alley at all."

"But he told you to leave the trash alone."

"If you think there's evidence in the sandwich wrappers that were rolling around the base of the Lewis & Clark statue, I apologize. But I think we both know that there wasn't, and now Main Street doesn't look like a ghetto."

The cop's look was displeased, but I tied the bag and set it outside the alleyway. "In case you want to get your *evidence,*" I said.

I didn't bother to wait for a reply and went into 2nd Chance to find the staff's addresses. I guessed that Zee would be the one to have the most accurate information. She seemed to have a way with people and knew everyone in town. She struck me as the town's crazy aunt.

What I found stopped me in my tracks.

❧ 8 ❧

My office had been a place that I hadn't explored much. Jenny had owned her diner for years, and the office showed it with boxes and shelves and dark corners that probably hadn't been updated, sorted, or cleaned out in years. Maybe even decades. One entire wall was covered with hefty filing cabinets and every time I looked at them I flinched. No doubt there were decades of bank statements and invoices in those. I'd had to shove one bookshelf in front of another in order to make room for Daisy's dog crate and food bowls, and emptying it had stirred up what felt like a century of dust and filled every available space, which made reshelving everything even more difficult. I'd shoved it all back without paying attention. Other than that all I'd added to the office were hooks on the back of my door for my coat, scarf, and bag.

Who wanted to take on clearing the office when there was the chance to pursue the more apparent and fun parts of their dreams? I'd focused instead on updating the look of the diner and learning how to cook the existing menu and deciding what recipes I'd perfected that I wanted to add. I spent much of my time shadowing Az and Zee, learning both their jobs. Jenny had taken a few hours to explain her process for paying employees, ordering food, and keeping records. I fully expected to stumble but hoped with Az's and Zee's help, I'd be able to keep things going. I didn't expect anything from Tara but her working hard after she showed up late.

Jenny had kept files on the employees, but it took me awhile to find them. While I searched for them, I found box upon box of notebooks. At first, I thought they were old employee files, but there were too many for that. They were also far, far more organized than I expected given the state of the office. The boxes weren't the details an employer needed with things like the social security number or record of a food handler's card.

They looked like different types of journals. I found one for Tara right off, on the top of the pile. Given how it was stuffed with so many "write-ups" for being tardy, I assumed Jenny was in this file daily. I flipped quickly through and then grabbed one of our take-out bags and placed the files inside.

A few minutes flipping, and I hadn't only found the file for Zee, I'd found one for Jane and Mattie and Simon and Paige and the bookstore owner. There were more beyond that. Whole boxes of names and dirt on the people of the town. My eyes were wide with shock of what I was finding. I grabbed Paige from the boutique's file and found that Jenny had documented Paige shorting Tara for lunch by leaving cash on the table. Paige had an affair with Henry from the bookshop even though she'd been married for twenty-two years. Paige had put some of her trash in the pizza shop's garbage when hers had been full and stiffed that guy with the larger trash bill since it had overfilled his. It was petty stuff and things that ended marriages—maybe even lives.

Kyle's file was all documented breakups and drug usage. Some thievery. Crimes. The kind that you did to buy drugs, not necessarily the kind of thing that was truly dangerous.

The random things I found, though—they were weird and petty. Not information that people would actually kill over. The fact the records existed, however, was horrifying. It made me realize as I read through it that Jenny, through the diner, had seen so much. She'd hadn't just seen, though, she'd pried into things and made nasty guesses and documented people's worst moments.

There was a file about some woman named Roberta who ran on the beach every morning. According to Jenny's calculations, it should have taken Roberta forty-five minutes to do her normal run, but she took an hour and half each day. I frowned. The woman was running on the beach, maybe she only slowed down to walk along the water or grab a few shells? It didn't make sense to even take note of this, but it had to Jenny. What a nosy old biddy. Jenny hadn't put conclusions to what she'd recorded, but I assumed because she hadn't decided what Roberta was up to.

I had liked Jenny so I was shocked by what I was finding. I wouldn't have expected this level of nosiness in the woman who had made me swear on my mother's grave to not fire her staff—not even Tara. My judgement of Jenny was faltering, and I was upset I'd been so off. I wanted to like her. I still wanted to. She'd been so protective of her staff. She'd made me repeat, "None of them. Not even Tara."

I grabbed Tara's file again and leaned back to read in more detail. There were nearly daily notes on Tara and Kyle. *Tara and Kyle broke up again. She's already softening on taking him back.* Or, *Tara was late again. I wasn't surprised when I saw Morgan lingering outside. Never did like that girl.* Or, *Tara spent the evening with Nathaniel Blake. If only she'd give that boy a chance.* I was suddenly desperate to know who Nathaniel Blake was, and I was super curious about Roberta as well.

Where were the files for the others? I dug through the entirety of the office until my legs were aching from standing and squatting, but I didn't find a file for Az. That concerned me more than I wanted it to. Az was my favorite of the diner crew. There had to have been a file, which meant...it meant...he either knew about the files and removed his or that Jenny, who protected no one else's secrets, protected Az's. I didn't even have his necessary information—his social security card, his food handler's card, his address—nothing.

And Tara...if the notes could be trusted, her relationship with Kyle was as rocky as I'd been told. Should I use that as some sort of proof that the rest of this stuff could be trusted? Maybe I should read the files on Simon, Jane, and Mattie to see what they said. If those files were right—

I would be furious if someone had read a file on me. I wanted to go find Zee, Az, and Tara, but I felt like I needed to know how trustworthy this information was or how damaging.

I debated for a few minutes, temptation, that alluring beast, *calling* to me to read Simon's file. No, I told myself. No, Rose. Don't do it. Don't ruin things. I felt as though I needed to have a cat on my lap instead of my Daisy. Curiosity and cats, right?

I finally stuffed everything into my bag, texted Mattie to ask her to lunch—I needed another perspective on this stuff—then headed out the door. As I locked up, I found Simon standing by my car.

I tried to be casual as I walked forward with my bag full of...what? Potential evidence? I popped the back of my car, set my bags casually inside, and closed it. How I hoped that I'd been casual enough.

He hadn't moved as I'd stowed my things, including those red flag files of gossip and meanness. I tried to smile, but I was so stressed out and he was here. Why? Because we were friends or for some other reason?

His arms were folded over his chest. "Kyle died."

Oh. Anger fled at that. I had expected Kyle's death, but I guess hope had been stronger than I'd realized. I wasn't sure what to do. Tell him what I'd found? No. I couldn't. I couldn't tell him about those files of gossip if it would get my team in trouble, so I needed to see what was in them first. Maybe if I actually found something. Of course, I'd tell him about a murderer, but I wasn't going to tell him about Paige or Tara, or the fact that Az didn't have a file. Not unless I couldn't help it. I wouldn't help him mess up their lives unless I had good reason to believe one of them was a killer.

"I'm sorry to hear that," I said. I felt like I should add, *He was a good kid.* Or, *We'll miss him.* But we both knew that those things would be hypocritical. Finally, I found something, "I'm sure he'll be missed. His poor family."

Simon nodded once, his jaw tight, and I suddenly realized that because the town was so small and given his role in it as a cop, he must have known Kyle. Simon must have known how many times Kyle had been arrested. Maybe Simon had driven him home to talk to his parents. Maybe Simon had found Kyle in the park too late or partying on the beach or at some late-night party drunk and needed his parents to try to stop that stuff.

"You knew him pretty well?" I asked.

Maybe I was reading into his relationship with the kid. But then Simon nodded once again, and I realized that he was having a hard time containing his emotions. And with that, I realized that I didn't know Simon very well. He was my friend, but we *were* new friends—this was the first time I'd seen him struggle. Let alone seen him mourn.

"Was he in trouble a lot?"

Simon sighed, nodded, then added, "We tried hard to turn him around. He was just so determined to be in trouble."

"It's not fair he didn't have time to grow up, to turn it around," I said. Suddenly the tragedy of Kyle's death was hitting me personally. Kyle *had* nearly hurt me, but he had been *young*. He didn't have the chance to mature, to fall in love, to find a life passion. He never found anything that was worth changing for, maybe a reason to be something more than a deadbeat. Maybe he would have found something to reward the faith, work, and love that people had put into him.

"I'm sorry," I said, hearing the truth in my voice. I was surprised that Simon's regret over Kyle was making my heart ache in a way that I wouldn't have expected. That morning I'd been offended that I was being investigated. Being a murder suspect made me angry. That Kyle was dead made me regret him in the most clichéd ways.

Perhaps my regret was enough to soften Simon because his attitude changed. He reached towards me, just a little bit, before pulling his hand back.

Then he shifted, stood taller, and asked, "Did you ever talk to Kyle again after the accident?"

Oh, I thought, oh my, that hurt. He had felt like a friend again, for a second. I knew he probably was a friend. I knew he was doing his job. That none of this was his fault, but it didn't feel that way. Especially when you added that he'd felt *maybe* something more for a moment. Just the swiftest, sweetest of moments. And following that with questions like these felt like a personal attack. A lack of faith. A rejection.

In that moment, I realized—there was only one way to take back my second chance, my friendships, what I wanted for my life in Silver Falls. It was to find out who killed Kyle and to *own* my second chance.

"No," I said, even more determined to protect my people, myself— my heart. I took a deep breath, reminded myself he was a police officer and tried to hide my disappointment and my determination. "No, I didn't see Kyle before the accident. I didn't see him until he walked into the diner. I didn't even know his name. I never looked for him or asked about him."

"Rose..." There was enough emotion in Simon's voice that made me think he might feel bad about my status as suspect. "I have to ask."

"Okay," I said, but I didn't feel okay about it. Of course, I didn't.

"I'll find the killer," Simon said. "It's my job."

It didn't escape me that the killer could be anyone. Including me. I was certain it hadn't escaped him either. Yes, I thought, you try to find the killer. And so will I.

❧ 9 ❧

Zee's place was at the end of a dirt road towards the farmland rather than the ocean. It was a tiny little cottage covered in roses, and there were actual rabbits in the garden and a white picket fence around the yard. It had taken me four times as long as it should have to get there because I'd taken several wrong turns, despite GPS, and been eyed by more than one judgmental, long-lashed, dairy cow.

I could see three cats in the front window of the cottage and another in the upper window. Every single thing about the mean, sharp-tongued, sarcastic grandma's house was sweet and adorable. It was the exact opposite, in fact, of Zee.

"I'm not working today," Zee said as I got out of the Forrester. She was sitting on an actual porch swing, drinking something steamy out of a cat cup where the tail was the handle. Zee was wearing a cute little plaid dress where her knobby knees showed, but her legs were strong, and her orthotic shoes somehow brought her outfit together rather than standing out. The matching compression socks somehow crossed it over into chic, quirky grandma.

"Oh, my gosh," I said. "You are the cutest gramma I ever saw. Ever. Look at you!"

She scowled, her eyes narrowing, her wrinkles accentuating her distaste. I couldn't help but grin.

"I'll quit right now and where will you be?"

"So screwed," I admitted placatingly. "The town loves you, the staff loves you, I love you. You know that restaurant and running it better than the rest of us put together. And far, far, far better than I do."

She coughed. "Well, all right then."

I walked through the gate and up to the house, hoping she'd understand what I was thinking and get behind my plan. And help me. I didn't think I could do this without her. No one would talk to me. I was the newb. But Zee...she was like everyone's mean old aunt that they still loved for no apparent reason.

"I need your help," I said precisely, knowing there was no way to get it outside of abject humility.

"Yes, I know."

"Not with the diner." I considered and added, "Not *just* with the diner. Also with finding Kyle Johannson's killer."

"He's dead?" She didn't wait for an answer but took another sip from her cup and looked me over. "That boy overdosed."

I shook my head.

I could see her consider, and her scowl deepening, but what she said was, "Why do you care what happened to him? He was a stupid boy who did nothing but cause destruction and pain. Those who care about him are better off now."

"He was poisoned," I said. I leaned against the balustrade of her porch across from her and said, "We're suspects, Zee. We handled the food. It happened at our diner."

"Ours?"

"Ours," I said. "You know 2nd Chance is as much yours as mine. You've worked there forever. You care about 2nd Chance—or Jenny's— whatever you want to call it. You care about it and you're a part of it. Of course, you are."

"Maybe I need a different life," Zee said, suddenly sounding tired. "Suspects? Murder? I don't want any part of that. That boy died? Jane didn't save him?"

I sighed. "I...Zee...oh goodness, Zee. They treated him for a drug overdose. They didn't realize what was happening until it was too late."

"And they think we did it?"

"He died over spaghetti and meatballs. Our spaghetti and meatballs."

Zee laughed a harsh, nasty laugh. "Spaghetti, meatballs, and murder. I delivered the food you know. They both asked for meatballs. Morgan was all excited about something. They were whispering together."

I hadn't known. I didn't doubt that it was true, but it seemed to make it all the more an unlikely murder. Could it have been an accident? But, of course not, you didn't accidentally slip someone your insulin. And none of us were diabetic. At least I didn't think so.

"Are you diabetic?"

"I'm healthy as a hundred horses," Zee snorted. She took another drink of her cup and then cleared her throat. "I'll be having coffee and scrambled eggs for breakfast when I hit a hundred."

"I wonder what the whispering was all about." I laid my head against the post and had to admit I was at a loss. "What was their secret? What could they have been excited about?"

Zee started to answer, then her shoulders dropped. "What I want to say seems wrong now, seeing how that stupid boy is dead."

I had to laugh even though I wasn't that amused. It was tragic. "Simon thinks I did it."

She snorted evilly before she answered. "No he doesn't."

"But he's asked me about it twice. *You* didn't even know Kyle was dead, and I've been interviewed two times."

Zee's expression was sour and mean—like usual. Her expression seemed to matter more than ever given the way she was eyeing me. "He cares about clearing your name, stupid girl. He likes you more than he's liked the other women on his long string of fawners."

"Other women? Long string? He does not like me more than his long string of women. Hah." I didn't sound amused, and I added, "Questioning me is no way to show it."

"Of course it is, stupid girl. Stupid, stupid girl. You're the new girl in town. Clearing you matters most. Only a few people know you or like you."

I frowned, hating that line of reasoning. I could see what she was saying. I wasn't stupid as much as she liked to call me that. I could see how the town would prefer me as the murderer even if I had less reason than anyone else to kill Kyle. The only connection between me and the kid was that accident, but that episode was something for people to cling to as far as my guilt went. After all, no one cared all that much about me. I wasn't anyone's school teacher or best friend or cousin's daughter. It would be easier for all of them if I had done it. Then everything could go back to how it had been before I bought Jenny's. Before I'd created my second chance. Before I'd found what felt like a new home.

I shook my head. "It doesn't feel that way. It doesn't feel like caring at all."

"Of course, it doesn't. You think he won't come on over here and question me? Of course Simon will. He'll ask me his questions, and I won't appreciate it one little bit. But he'll ask me. No one will believe I'm the killer though. They know me. I'd have been far more likely to take that boy by his ear, walk him to the counter at the diner, and fill his foul mouth with hot sauce."

"So you want to team up and figure this out with me?" I asked, crossing my fingers behind my back.

"Why do I need you?" Her brows rose, and there was no doubting the challenge in her question.

"You don't. I need to clear my name more than you do, so I'm going to figure this out regardless. I suppose though—" I smiled wickedly, knowing she'd hate what I was going to say, "—if I get arrested, the diner will close."

I was right. Her already irritated expression deepened into near rage. But her voice didn't change a bit. "Don't you trust Simon?"

I had to consider for a moment. "Yes. This is my new life. I won't risk everything I'm working for. Not on blind faith towards someone that I don't know nearly well enough yet."

"So you don't trust him."

"I trust him," I said, struggling to explain. "I trust him to do everything he can. I trust him to try. I won't stop beating myself up in jail if I don't at least try, though. Don't I owe it to myself to clear my name?"

Zee didn't reply, but her gaze was heavy on me.

So I added the thing I thought would get her to help. "And I owe it to try to clear the names of our diner family."

"Smooth," she said. "I don't need you."

I waited, hoping. There had been something in how she said it that gave me a shred of hope.

"But I don't need you fouling things up either."

"Okay," I said, humbly, trying to hold back anything that might set Zee off.

She glanced me over. "You better not be the killer."

I couldn't help but gasp, but she didn't care that she'd hurt my feelings.

"I suppose you're either a crazy killer or you're innocent. Though there's not much of a reason for someone like you to kill that stupid boy."

"Thanks for the vote of confidence," I said.

She looked over and I realized that I heard the sound of a car. "Go inside," she said. "Eavesdrop if you must, but don't come out until he's gone."

I obeyed, even though I was dying of curiosity. I slid through the door before I was seen. Whoever she'd seen was out of sight behind bushes now, and they'd see me soon if I stayed outside. I made my way into her house and paused in sheer, unadulterated horror. Everywhere I looked I found ceramic cats with eyes that seemed to follow me. I was convinced they'd be sucking out my soul if I stayed too much longer, but I heard the slam of a car door and dropped to the ground before I was seen. Then I remembered that my car was sitting front and center in the drive. But there was nothing I could do about it.

Just as heavy boots hit the porch outside, a long-haired, orange tabby cat came around the corner of Zee's...goodness, it could only be called a parlor. Zee had a maroon settee and those hardback chairs with a sort of velvet fabric. They were all covered in plastic, probably to keep the cat hair off, and it couldn't have been any less creepy covered in sheets and cobwebs. There was *something* about all those ceramic cats.

"Where is she?"

Was he here looking for me?

"Picking the last of the apple crop," I heard Zee say. Thank goodness she'd thought of a way to explain my car. "She's experimenting with some apple cheese pie or some other such nonsense. As if anyone wants anything other than apple pie with ice cream like we've always served. Girl's a fool."

Simon cleared his throat and I closed my eyes to focus on what he was saying, and, of course, to avoid those cats.

"It's not all bad," he said. "That chocolate layer cake is heavenly. I have to admit though that apple cheese thing sounds nasty."

"You always did have a sweet tooth, stupid boy," Zee said meanly. "Got your head turned by layer cakes and how sweet she is."

He didn't touch that comment, but my face flamed. I was happy no one could see it.

"She tell you about Kyle?"

"Course she did. She's not a big fan of you focusing your investigation on her. Better be careful boy or the first woman who's captured your eye will move right beyond you. You aren't the only one with eyes and taste buds."

"Now, Zee," Simon said pleadingly, "Rose isn't...I'm just...it's my job."

Zee snorted that mean snort of hers. "Sure. Keep lying to yourself, but I saw Jeb Mason eyeing her the other day. He won't believe she killed Kyle, I can tell you that much."

"I *don't* believe she killed Kyle," Simon said, and I believed him. I *believed* him, and it was a shining sun in my chest that warmed me through and through. I cracked open my eyes and leapt in my skin. Three cats were sitting in front of my feet, circling me as if they were deciding where they would begin eating me.

"Oh goodness," I whispered, choking back a shriek.

"Then why do you keep interviewing her?" Zee asked as I tried not to freak out.

"She isn't the only one I've been interviewing, and quite frankly you all might have seen something. You all might have been unwitting deliverers of the poison."

"It was my table," Zee said. "I served those two idiots."

"You don't sound very sad that he's dead."

"Being dead does not change Kyle being an idiot nor does grieving make Morgan any less of a two-faced fool."

"Zee, you've always had a way with words. Now that you know it was murder, did you see anything?"

"Yeah, I saw a lot of things. I saw Tara avoiding the table because Kyle was a cheating dog and Morgan was a no-good betraying piece of trampery. I saw Hector Allen talk Tara into giving him an extra-large piece of cake and not paying for it either. I saw four tables that were out of drinks, I saw a pile of cash on table four, which wasn't there when I swung by to pick it up. I saw my job. Or did you mean did I see anyone jab Kyle in the neck with a needle or put something shady in his food? No, of course I didn't. I'd have said something to the boy if I had. None of this would ever have happened."

Simon cleared his throat and tried again, "But there wasn't anyone hanging around the table?"

"Simon, when it's busy like that, you can't focus on whether someone is lingering around a table. You're moving your behind getting the glasses filled, scanning for anything that is wrong or anybody needing ketchup. You aren't looking for *poisoners,* you're looking for someone who needs more iced tea. I bet Az could tell you how many meatballs we went through. I bet Tara could tell you how many steps she walked and whether she changed the diet coke syrup, but the point is that we were working. And we were working harder than we have in a while. None of us were paying attention to that table."

Simon oomphed. "This isn't a personal attack, Zee. Maybe you know something you don't realize."

"Have you talked to Morgan? They came in together. She was at the table with him."

"Of course I have. She and Kyle both left to go to the bathroom. She swears he wasn't using. At least that she could tell. She didn't see anyone do anything to the food."

"And does the autopsy bear that out?" Zee's doubt in the question made it clear just what she thought of Morgan's reliability.

"It's too soon to say," Simon said. "You sound a little too much like *Murder She Wrote*. You pumping me for information, Zee?"

Zee snorted again. "I'm concerned that you sound a little too much like *The Pink Panther*. Normally you have domestic disturbance calls and drunk drivers. You up for this?"

I winced for Simon and scrunched up my nose, watching the cats watch me. One of them seemed to narrow its eyes at me, and it made me want to crawl backwards, but I wasn't supposed to be listening, and I didn't want to be found. What would Simon think if he found me like this?

I crawled forward and made my way down the hall. The room at the end of the hall was the kitchen, and I glanced around. What I saw paused me completely. It was an ancient, perfectly maintained, green linoleum with green countertops, white cabinets, china cat cookie jars, and bran muffins sitting on the countertop.

The front door opened and I darted out the back door in the kitchen. I found a basket of apples outside the door. Zee must have been picking apples before I got there. I grabbed it, took a deep breath, then I opened the back door. I saw Simon and Zee, who eyed the basket of apples and winked at me.

"Hey." I feigned a surprised look to see him and waited for his hey, which didn't come. "Seeing if Zee killed the kid?" I didn't wait for an answer. "Stress baking. I'm thinking apple and cheese pie."

"Ooh, yeah. That sounds good," Simon lied.

I grinned. I was going to make so many cheese and apple pies and serve them up to him. I could see a cheese and apple pie with a candle on it in my head for his birthday. I wasn't sure how long I'd torture him, but I was definitely going to torture him for a while. Maybe forever. Even if things worked out between us, I was pretty sure I was going to make so many cheese and apple pies that the mere smell would make him flinch.

I met Zee's gaze and it was as if she could read my mind. She gave me one nod. "You'll do."

Simon glanced at her and then back at me.

I got a wicked wink after that, and I smiled innocently at him.

"So you two are going to be cooking pie today?" Simon asked. "Good."

Zee smiled, but Simon wasn't looking her way as he left the cottage. She'd have given us away if Simon had seen that wicked, snide smirk.

She snorted in an amused sort of way the second he was in his car, and we both waved as he drove away. Zee jerked her head towards my car, and I realized she was dismissing me.

"I thought we were going to investigate," I said.

She snorted again and I frowned at her.

I had more questions, so I paused before I opened the car door. Daisy barked from the front seat, but I ignored her to ask, "Did you know about the files that Jenny kept? On everyone?"

"Course I did."

"Why didn't you clear your file out?"

Zee grinned evilly. "Well, that would have been obvious. I have nothing to hide."

"Did you take Az's file?"

"Who me?"

Her face was utterly innocent, but I wasn't sure I could believe it. Not at all. Especially with the way she'd said 'who me?' She might be wearing compression socks and orthotics, but there was nothing slow or elderly about the way she eyed me. I couldn't be sure if she was covering for Az taking his own file, or if she was hiding something. Maybe Jenny had hidden whatever she knew about Az. But why would Jenny protect only Az?

"I don't think he killed Kyle," I said with a tone that invited explanation.

"Why would he?" Zee asked, and there was no question about the challenge in her voice or the fact that she wasn't going to be telling me a single thing. "Az is a good man."

I thought about all the missing information on Az, about the way he'd big brothered Tara, and I had to wonder if he had anything to do with Kyle's death. It seemed...possible. He was protective. He was kind and he was good and he was a hard worker, and I liked him a *lot*. But, it seemed possible. I suppose if you worked hard enough at it, any of us could be the killer, and I didn't buy it.

I didn't say anything but Zee seemed to read my thoughts. "Don't be stupid, Rose."

"I didn't say anything."

"You thought it."

"Az is a good man," I said. It was all I said, and it meant a lot of different things. It meant that I like him and trust him and that I could see him protecting Tara. If Az knew something about Kyle, and if it were bad enough, I could see what might have happened. A startling realization came to me about the laid-back cook, something about him that said he'd do what had to be done and that he loved fiercely.

But to be honest, making me think about this made me realize I could see a dark side of myself too. I suppose I wanted to think that I wouldn't do the same. And perhaps what was saddest of all is that there was only one person I would be so very dangerous for. That made me sad.

"Who would you kill for?" I asked Zee.

She was a smart woman. Much savvier than you'd guess from seeing her deliver plates of pancakes and harassing the town people.

"Not very many people," she said.

She didn't ask me who I'd kill for and I was grateful for it. My mom. That was it. And even then it was hard to imagine. How lonely my life had become before my second chance here. I had made better friends in the few weeks I'd lived in Silver Falls than I had in all my years answering phone calls.

"Do we need to talk to Az?"

"Will you be happy if we don't?"

I thought about it for a moment before I shook my head.

"I want to be making cake today." I sighed, glancing around her beautiful yard with the cats in the window and the trees in the back. The grass in the fields surrounding the cottage was high, and it smelled fresh and amazing, like countryside with a tinge of sea salt. "And to be considering the next event night. And not having my life ruined by the murder of some poor kid."

"I'll talk to Az with you later. Tomorrow," Zee said. "Out girl. I'm going to bring cookies to Kyle's mother and see what I can find out. Maybe he was suicidal. Maybe he stole drugs from some relative and took insulin by mistake. That wouldn't be surprising, would it? We'll talk to Az tomorrow. Be to work early. Az'll be there chopping and dicing."

❧ 10 ❧

I rolled down the window as Daisy and I drove away and let the wind run over my skin. She stuck her little head out the window, standing on her back legs and letting her tongue loll. The smell of the ocean and the rain filled the car. I picked up my phone and saw that Mattie had texted me back. I had invited her to lunch and she was game. I wasn't sure what to expect from lunch since I had her and Jane's file hidden under a blanket in the back of the car.

It took way less time to reach downtown Silver Falls, and I pulled up outside the spa, wishing I had thought to message Jane or have Mattie do it.

"Hey," I said as Mattie opened the car door and jumped inside. "When's your next appointment?"

She glanced over, raised her brows, and said, "Three."

Given the expression on her face, she'd picked up on my layered thoughts. My mind was going a thousand miles an hour, and everything was askew.

"How would you feel about Blackfish?"

"In Lincoln City?"

I nodded. "I have some things to say."

"As long as there will be drinks."

"You think Jane is available?"

Mattie pulled out her phone. She spoke for a moment to Jane, then turned to me and said, "She's coming."

I drove towards the clinic and grabbed Jane, then I dropped Daisy off at my cottage. I opened the back of the car and grabbed the files before climbing back into the driver's seat. I handed them both a file and pulled away from the cottages.

"What's going on?" Jane asked as she opened her file. She paused as she glanced over the papers. "What the...?" She flipped through the file. "Have you read this?"

I glanced over as I drove down Highway 101 and admitted, "I wanted to."

"But you didn't?" Her voice was shaking, and I was desperate to know what she was worried about. But curiosity didn't just kill cats—it killed friendship, and I liked Jane enough to let her have her secrets.

"I didn't," I said. I glanced into the review mirror and saw that her gaze was fixated on the file, which was trembling in her hands.

She looked up and met my gaze, but I had to repeat myself when I saw the look in her eyes. "Jane," I said gently, "I did *not* read your file."

I glanced at Mattie. "Either of your files."

Mattie tossed hers into her purse. "My mom would tell you most of this stuff."

There was something in her voice that said that the file had some things that her mom wouldn't know.

"Was she wrong about any of it?" I asked.

"Was it Jenny? *Why* does she have these?" Jane asked. "Has anyone else seen this?"

I took a breath and slowed as I drove into Lincoln City. Blackfish Cafe was right off the main drag and easy to spot with the skeletal fish on the side of the dark grey building.

"I went into 2nd Chance to find the employee files and came across a lot of these. It's not only you. As far as I can tell, it's anyone who piqued Jenny's interest."

"And she just left them behind?"

I nodded. "I read the one on Tara and Zee, but I wasn't sure what to believe. So, when I saw your names, I thought I could give them to you and see if what was in there was true."

"But you didn't read it?" Jane's voice was stringent, but I realized that Mattie wasn't surprised. Did she know whatever Jane wanted hidden? "Why would she keep these? Why would Jenny make them, keep them, and then…then…just leave them? What if you were horrible?"

I didn't expect the question, but the fact that it existed made me sad. They were the closest things I had to friends, and I want to be trusted.

"I didn't read it," I said clearly and precisely. "I didn't even open them. Either of them."

Jane's hands were still shaking as she began meticulously tearing up the file.

Mattie and I waited until Jane was done before going into the restaurant. Jane headed to the bathroom while we were seated, and I immediately ordered a drink for each of us entirely chosen by the name—Manhattan Mission. I didn't know what it was, but it sounded like something Jane could use as soon as she returned to the table.

I ordered myself a cup of clam chowder to help sop up the booze. I didn't need to look at the menu. I wanted scallops and that was all I needed to know. If they came wrapped in bacon that would be okay too.

Jane was back a few minutes later, and she took a long sip of her drink before she said, "It isn't…it's only my secret, you know? It isn't anything I would kill over."

I nodded and took a bite of my soup. I didn't want to drink on an empty stomach, so I hurried through my chowder even though it was my favorite ever.

"I didn't think you killed Kyle. I never even considered it," I said. "I was going to talk to my staff about the fact that Kyle died and that we were suspects. I was looking for employee addresses, not what I found."

"Who *does* that?" Jane demanded, taking another large drink of her Manhattan as though to wash down the idea. "Why would anyone keep files like those? Even if you had figured out what people were hiding, why would you write it down where anyone could read it?"

I glanced at Mattie, who was paler and determinedly putting away her own drink.

"What concerns me," I said, "is not finding a file for some people. People who you'd think would have one. I might go back in and arrange things. I don't want to keep them, but until the murderer is found, I'll be locking the office and waiting to see if…maybe…I don't know. I don't want to read people's secrets, but I feel like with the diner and the people who work there under the microscope, I'm not sure I can set those files aside."

Mattie and Jane were silent for a moment. Mattie glanced down at her bag where her file was poking out. Jane didn't answer, but she drained the rest of her drink. When the waitress came back, Jane ordered chowder, coffee, and another drink. I didn't say anything even though I was worried for her. Whatever that file brought to the front of Jane's mind took away the carefree, kind doctor and brought out someone who seemed to need a dose or two of anxiety meds and possibly a good run to work out some stress.

"What do you know about Az?" I asked Jane specifically because I thought she could use the distraction.

She blinked for a minute. "He's quiet. Good cook. Jenny's Diner really improved when he started working there. It was good before, but it got better."

I played with my spoon and finally took my own sip of my Manhattan. It was lovely, and I enjoyed it as I considered what to say next. I glanced between the two of them and realized that I trusted them with Az.

"He doesn't have a file," I said. "I asked Zee about it. She left me with the idea that she might have taken it."

"Why would she? She didn't take hers, right?" Mattie's finger was tapping against her glass.

"Right," I said. "But I read hers. Zee is what she is. She's not hiding anything except a terrifying ceramic cat collection."

Mattie snorted and finished her drink. We ordered our actual meals from the waitress and Jane seemed to calm down. I was sure she was stressed, but given that I wasn't acting any differently, she either accepted that I knew her secret and was okay with it or I hadn't read her file.

"Why are you investigating this?" Jane asked. She sounded a little perturbed. "Don't you trust Simon?"

"I have spent the vast majority of the last few years saving up and working towards what I have at 2nd Chance," I said, avoiding the subject that I had been very lucky in inheriting money. "This is something that I can't ignore. It could ruin my business."

Jane ordered a third Manhattan as our food was delivered and then, once the waitress left, said, "That won't happen."

I didn't bother arguing. She had the history of being a long-time resident of the town that I didn't have. Just because she and Mattie had accepted me quickly didn't mean that the rest of Silver Falls had. Besides, it wasn't only me, it was Az and Zee and Tara who I cared about. It was the people I hoped to hire soon who'd benefit from a job in a seasonal small town. It was Daisy, and my mom who were trusting me to find happiness.

I sipped my drink and played with my plate. The scallops were amazing but talking about murder and secrets had left my stomach upset. I was craving my kitchen and the calm that comes from baking and playing with recipes. I hated, *hated,* HATED that things had come to this and that this poor kid died.

But what I was realizing I hated, even more, was that it was really messing with my life. It was bad enough that he died, and I wanted to shout about how it was ruining things for me, but I didn't want to be that person. It made me feel like such a *jerk* to be inconvenienced by a kid's death. Except that I didn't necessarily feel inconvenienced. I felt like a tragedy was pushing itself into my life and threatening my happiness.

Goodness Rose, I thought, stop it.

We finished our subdued lunch, and as we got back into the car, Mattie said, "It's accurate. You want to know if Jenny's files were right. As far as I go, they were spot on."

"I didn't read it," I told Mattie again, but I glanced beyond her to Jane.

"We know," Mattie said. "I have an appointment. Let's head back."

I pulled a U-turn from our street spot and we went north towards Neskowin and Silver Falls. When I dropped them off, I went to get Daisy and we returned to 2nd Chance. I had a lot to think through, and I wanted to talk to both Tara and Az, but I thought they'd be more comfortable if Zee were there. And truthfully, I thought that Zee would keep the others from hedging. She knew both of them, and if she thought they were involved in a murder, she wouldn't protect them. But if we had a united front, maybe they'd feel safe?

I thought about how much I hated being questioned, and I doubted it. Regardless, I sent a text to everyone asking them to come early. Az replied within minutes, Zee replied with a curse word, and Tara didn't reply at all.

11

I finished making three cakes for the diner around midnight. I made a carrot, a triple chocolate, and a lemon and raspberry chiffon. They were all towering layer cakes, and I started to feel a little better when I began frosting the last of them. It was so soothing to spread buttercream around and watch the lazy susan move against the force of the still knife. Each cake was taller than the last, and the details were extra amazing in sugared flowers and a pile of fresh raspberries. I very much should have gone to bed before I made them. I needed to be to the diner by 5:30 am, but I couldn't sleep. I hadn't even intended to bake, but I couldn't settle my mind. Every time I closed my eyes, I saw Kyle dead, except he always seemed to land right into a plate of meatballs with his dead eyes staring at the ceiling.

I was never quite sure in those horrible little dreams if the red by his mouth was spaghetti sauce or blood, but either way, in the dark I was not sure I'd ever be able to eat spaghetti again. I decided in the darkness to take spaghetti off the menu for a while, which made me sad. It had been one of the recipes I'd first played with back in my tiny apartment when I'd been trying to find joy in anything. Anything at all. Taking it off the menu didn't make me as sad as Kyle's death, but I regretted it all the same. The 2nd Chance Diner was being tainted by what had happened, and it should be. It *should* be, but I wasn't sure how to reconcile my mourning over the diner with the mourning over the kid.

When I got back to my cottaged, I flopped onto my back and stared up at the ceiling. It had become home, and I loved it. Given that I'd rented it for only six months, I needed to make some other living choices, but I didn't want to. I loved the little cottage. I loved the window cracked with the sound of the waves and the wind, the smell of sea salt. It was as if the scent of rain never faded with the ocean just outside.

I tapped my feet against each other, and my legs were wiggling against my will. The cottage bedding had been replaced by my own, and I snuggled into the Egyptian cotton sheets, flopping my arm over my eyes as if that would help. It didn't. I rose, and it was so cold, I slipped my tennis shoes on.

In the kitchen, I started a pot of chamomile tea and grabbed my coat to ward off the chill in the air. But after a moment, I turned off the burner. Daisy had followed me faithfully to the kitchen and was watching me from the little bed I'd put in the corner.

"Want to go outside?"

She blinked sleepily at me, but when I grabbed the leash, she came trotting over.

"Hey," I said to her. "Maybe some sea air is just what we need."

I scoffed at myself at that one. I walked out of the cottage and stepped onto the dirt path between the beachfront property and the little paths that made their way down to the sandy beaches. I randomly selected going towards the moon. It was fall, and therefore the off-season. Given it was also a weekday, I could very well have been the only person around.

It was a little lonely. Maybe it should have been creepy, but it was peaceful. In Gresham and Portland, you never felt alone. Silver Falls wasn't nearly so crowded. I took deep breaths and tried to think sleepy thoughts as we walked, hoping that stretching my legs would get the wiggles and antsy feelings out.

It wasn't working, so I found a rock and sat on it. Daisy pawed my knee until I lifted her into my arms. I closed my eyes, letting the wind wash away the feel of the day and my worries.

"What are you doing out here?"

I looked up. There was a woman in the darkness, and I couldn't see her face.

"Just going for a walk," I said. "I'm a little..."

I trailed off, and there was a mean grunt. I couldn't help but glance over, surprised. I searched the darkness, but I couldn't make out a face.

"What you are doing is trespassing." She flicked a flashlight on and shined it right onto my face.

I flinched back and tried to escape it, but every time I turned away, she followed me with it.

"Hey," I said. "Could you stop?"

"I think not," she said. I could barely make out the additional light of a phone, and then I could hear the sound of ringing. There was an answer a moment or two later, and I realized the stupid woman actually called me in for trespassing.

"There," she said with the snide voice of someone who had probably been prom queen and had never forgotten. "We don't appreciate your kind in Silver Falls."

"What kind is that?" I gasped. I was about as white bread and boring as they came. I didn't appreciate the sentiment, but the mere idea that I was somehow offensive was ridiculous.

"I think you know," she said.

"Dog owners?" I asked. "Bakers? People who are thinking of taking up *knitting?*"

"I'm not unaware that Kyle Johansson died in your diner."

"From insulin poisoning," I said. "Not from choking on a meatball. *I* certainly didn't hurt him.'

She laughed a cruel, cold laugh. "That remains to be seen though doesn't it?"

I glanced to the side, waiting for whoever was going to come. I certainly wasn't going to try to run off after the woman called the police. Especially since I hadn't done anything wrong.

I heard the sound of a crunch of gravel before a large industrial flashlight was blinding me even further.

"Rose?" a deep, familiar voice asked.

I felt a flash of relief followed by worry. I was glad Simon had answered, but I was also worried that he had answered. Why was he working so late? Or perhaps this was one of his ladies and she'd called him because he was who she called. My goodness, was that a flash of jealousy? I realized it was and compartmentalized the thought for later examination.

"Simon?" I was squinting away from the light, shading my eyes, and he lowered the light to my feet.

"What are you doing here?"

"Walking off my sleeplessness," I told him, wishing that his presence made me feel safe and not jealous. Neither of those things were true.

"Here?"

Apparently, I should know where here was.

"I took the path outside the cottages," I said, frustration coloring my tone. "I walked towards the moon for more light. I don't even know where I am."

He cleared his throat, and I could see he was fighting to hold back his real feelings, regardless of what they were. "You're behind Mayor Roberta Jenkins house, Rose."

"Is the path private property? Why does it matter where I am? I was sitting watching the stars and thinking."

"No," Simon said as the mayor replied, "Yes."

Simon cleared his throat. "You're certainly close to the mayor's property line but given the circumstances...."

"It's late for some stranger to be prying around private residences. This *woman* doesn't have any reason to be outside of my house that isn't suspicious."

"Going for a sleepless walk isn't suspicious, Roberta," Simon said evenly. He sounded as if he were holding back a snap of anger. That anger didn't remove my jealousy.

"That's not how I see it," she snapped. "You need to take her in and question her more thoroughly about why she's here, and while you're at it about the poor druggie boy too."

The druggie boy? Geez, I thought. But I held my tongue on purpose. I wanted to see how this played out.

"Rose doesn't have any motive to have killed Kyle," Simon said. There was less hiding of the anger in his voice that time around, but he still sounded professional.

"Everyone heard about that accident, detective," Roberta said, making 'detective' sound like 'servant.'

"And yet she didn't press charges or even make a formal complaint."

"We all heard about her rage after it," the mayor countered.

"Anyone would have been rightfully upset at nearly being killed, Mayor," Simon said. "It isn't a legitimate reason to investigate her for the murder, and there's no evidence supporting that she did."

The mayor's tone had morphed to full chill when she said, "But it's not like you have evidence of anything, do you? Are you sure you're capable of investigating this matter?"

"Of course, I am," Simon said evenly. His voice was a perfectly respectful snap and he continued, "I will not arrest a woman for walking past your house, Mayor. Rose, let's go."

"Don't let your affection for a new pair of legs distract you from your job. Or you won't be serving here much longer."

"And yet," Simon said, "while I do serve, I'll be upholding the law, not your whims, Roberta."

He took hold of my arm, and I let him lead me away. I didn't particularly like being led around like a stray dog, but given that the mayor wanted to have me arrested for the baloney version of trespassing, I let it go.

"Rose," Simon said as we arrived at his truck, "you need to be careful."

"From what?" I snapped. "From the Silver Falls mass murderer? Please."

"There *is* a murderer out there," he said. I could see his shadow push his hair back and he sounded exhausted. I was glad I couldn't meet his eyes as I wasn't sure I wouldn't give in to his pleas and forget why I was upset.

"And it's convenient for *me* to be around to be the killer, isn't it? I'm everyone's favorite bad guy. If the new girl is the killer, no one is inconvenienced."

My fury was pouring out. Probably because I was so tired. Maybe because I was so hurt. Definitely because his doubt was more painful than I wanted it to be.

He stepped closer to me, reaching past me to open the passenger truck door. As he did, the light from the truck poured out.

"It isn't convenient for me," he said. Instead of stepping back, he leaned into me, cupping my cheek. "I don't like it at all."

His gaze fixed on my face. Or maybe it was my lips? I wasn't sure, I just knew that the chill of the evening had suddenly become far more apparent. There seemed to be a spark between us—maybe it was electricity? Chemistry? I knew that I wanted to step closer to him, but I was too proud for that. He considered me a possible killer, and I wasn't going to take one step closer until I was sure that *he* had no doubts left. And maybe not then.

I admitted to myself that his defending me had warmed me. That it made me feel better about him and about things between us, whatever they were, but I also admitted to myself that it wasn't quite enough. Not for this new, bright life that I was trying to build. I couldn't let my dreams be demeaned by suspicions, and I wouldn't be seen that way. I wouldn't be seen as a possible killer. Not by the man I had been hoping would be far, far more than a good friend.

I cleared my throat and slid to the side, away from his truck.

"Let me give you a ride home," he said, gently.

"I think I'll finish walking off my sleeplessness," I said. "On the sidewalk. Thanks for not arresting me."

His laugh was mean when he said, "As if I would arrest anyone for walking on the path that people walk by the beach. I'm no one's flunky."

"Don't lose your job," I said, setting Daisy down. She immediately pawed Simon's foot for a pet, and he obliged.

"Duke misses his friend," Simon said.

I was sure the dog did. They'd played together nearly every day since we both adopted our dogs. They'd have to get over it.

"Have a good night," I said because I didn't have anything else to say. Not right then. But I promised myself I'd do whatever I could to return my life to the path it had been on. The one with good friends and the one with a possible love and the one with an excellent diner that I was loving running.

"Rose?"

I had turned away, but I glanced back over my shoulder.

"I'm going to find the real killer," he said.

The fact that he used the word "real" made me appreciate him a whole lot more, but I didn't react other than to say, "That sounds good."

"And then we're gonna have words."

There was enough warmth in his voice that I was very much looking forward to those words.

"Okay," I said.

"Text me when you get home?" he asked and because he asked so nicely I nodded.

I headed back towards the cottage, made my tea while texting Simon, and finally slipped into a dreamless sleep.

🐿 12 🐿

"Hey everyone," I said brightly. I slapped a paper bag down on the counter and grinned at them as I pulled out a five-hour energy drink and some eye drops. I chugged the drink and then glanced around again. "No Tara?"

"Did you expect her to be on time?" Zee asked snidely. She started a pot of coffee. "You know better than that."

I took a deep breath, admitted to myself that I'd hoped, and then lied. "Not really."

"Liar," Zee said. She poured herself a cup of coffee from the pot she'd made, then poured one for Az, too.

"One for me, please," I said.

Zee glanced me over, eyed the empty energy drink, and said, "Too much caffeine will kill you."

Az said nothing, but he started pouring out pancakes. We'd made it a habit to have a pancake breakfast when we had our morning meetings. They sounded good and the smell filled the diner immediately.

"We're suspects for the murder, Az," Zee announced as if she were saying that it would rain later that day. She added cream and sugar to her coffee.

"I figured we would be," he said. He poured another row of

pancakes and threw down a bag of hash browns. He flipped the row of pancakes and added the brown sugar topping in a swirl that turned them into cinnamon roll pancakes.

"Did you? I was surprised," I admitted, and even I heard the sadness in my voice. I grabbed the eye drops, putting them in my burning, exhausted eyes, and hoped they'd hide whatever emotion was welling there too.

"We served the food that was poisoned," he said simply. He cleared his throat and added butter onto the hash browns before cracking eggs to fry for us. It would be a breakfast to slow us down, counteracted by the work to do and the caffeine we'd swill. "There's no way we'll avoid being questioned."

His voice sounded sad, and I examined his face. Nothing more than regret seemed to reflect on those features. He knew why I was studying him, and his dark brown eyes crinkled at me—completely not offended that I was searching for hidden secrets or motives.

"Kyle was an idiot. He was cruel and petty and mean and very young," Az said. "I'd have happily kicked him out of the diner and out of Tara's life, but that wasn't my choice to make."

He was answering the questions I didn't want to ask, and he was doing it without an ounce of a grudge. I realized in a flash I should probably cut Simon some slack. I smiled at Az. His voice was rumbly and rich, and I liked it very much. What I liked more was the emotion behind those words. Any doubts I had about Az and Kyle were gone.

"Goodness, I want this to be over. We need that murderer found before people stop coming to the diner and start really suspecting us."

Az started serving up stacks of pancakes, putting too much butter on mine just how I liked them and no butter at all on Zee's. I shook my head at her as she took her first bite of her dry, plain pancakes.

I poured the cream cheese topping all over my pancakes, far, far, too heavily for good health, and I took a far too large bite for anything but a rabid animal.

"So you didn't kill Kyle," Zee told Az. "I didn't. Rose doesn't know enough about Kyle to truly hate him as he deserved. Did you see anything? All I can remember is far, far too many meatballs for any one person to serve."

"Nope," Az said. "Me and Eddie just served up plate after plate of spaghetti and tried to keep things flying. I'm not sure I saw anything other than the plates of food."

"You talk to the police yet?" Zee asked.

He glanced at her and back at the grill and suddenly I was suspicious. There was something in that look that said they knew a secret I didn't.

Oh goodness no, I thought. Please no. Not my staff. Not my diner. Not my second chance.

"Eddie did while I was out fishing yesterday," Az said. "He has a job on a fishing boat, so he's out for a few weeks. Hopefully, they don't need to talk to him again."

His voice was utterly peaceful and calm. Just a deep rumble of information, but his glance at Zee said something far, far more. If I hadn't been paying attention, I wouldn't have even noticed. But the first time, I'd looked up at the right time. I shoved my plate of pancakes away and ignored the smaller plate with hash browns and eggs.

My head cocked as I glanced between them, and I considered. *Why* would either of them kill the local drugged-out teen? They wouldn't. How could they have a motive? Even if they hated him, you didn't kill over hating your coworker's boyfriend. You just didn't. Zee worked at the diner, spent her afternoons with friends, and her evenings with her cats. She was a sassy local crone who enjoyed living here and interacting with the town. She'd no more have killed Kyle than I would have. If anything, she'd have harassed him until he avoided her relentlessly.

Az made even less sense. For a while there, I'd seen him as a protector, but I didn't think that was the case. I didn't think, as much affection as he might have for Tara, that Az would have removed Kyle from *life.* Maybe, *maybe,* Az would have given Kyle a good beating. Far more likely, Az would have threatened the kid without actually lifting a finger. Az was a huge man with wide shoulders and something that said his life had been rough. He'd have terrified Kyle with mere insinuations.

It didn't make sense. But *what* were they hiding?

"Something wrong with the pancakes?" Az's deep, Jamaican accent rolled through the kitchen, and I shook my head even as I stood and scraped my plates into the trash can.

"Too much caffeine, I guess," I lied.

"Told you," Zee said with her usual mean tone.

I tried smiling at them. "Well, I guess we should get to it."

I crossed into the office, checked on Daisy, and submitted my grocery order. When I came back out, Zee had turned the sign and only Simon, Jane, and Mattie were sitting in the diner. Usually, Henry, the paper delivery guy, came in for coffee and toast before heading to his second job. I narrowed my eyes. Across the street at the tiny little coffee shop, there was a line out the door. I ground my teeth in frustration. We'd lost our early regulars to a tiny shop without enough seating.

I closed my eyes and crossed to my friends, taking their order.

"Tara here yet?" Simon asked casually. Not casually enough for me to miss that he wanted to *talk* to her.

I shook my head and walked into the kitchen rather than to the order window.

"They want pancakes. Make one an order of buckwheat pancakes and scrambled egg whites, sliced tomatoes, grilled asparagus and mushrooms."

Az looked up, glanced out at the table and asked, "Who decided to be healthy?"

I shrugged and his eyes narrowed on me. I gave him my evilest smirk before pulling out a tub of tomatoes to begin slicing for later that day.

"You're playing with fire," Az told me. "You have his attention already. What are you going to do when he realizes you're more than a new, pretty face?"

Simon *had* ordered cinnamon roll pancakes, 2 fried eggs over easy, bacon, and hash browns.

"What do you think him realizing that will do?" I put a tomato in the slicer, shoved the blade over, then did another.

"I think you'll fixate his attention and have to decide what you want out of him. Because he's going to figure out what he wants from you."

I glanced over at him, shook my head, then processed several more tomatoes before I asked, "And what's that?"

Az's deep chuckle preceded his answer, "Everything you'll give him."

I snorted and finished the tub of tomatoes as Az finished serving up the plates. I took them up, grabbing a serving of the berry compote, leaving the butter off and arranging Simon's plate to be the healthiest version of food we offered. He'd hate it. I couldn't help but grin at Az before lifting the tray and heading out the kitchen door to hand out the plates.

I gave Jane her cinnamon roll pancakes first, then Mattie her crunchy French toast and finally handed Simon the remains. He glanced down and then up at me. Given they were our only customers, there was no chance I'd messed up his order. He narrowed his eyes at me, and I smiled brightly. As if I didn't see anything wrong, filling up his coffee cup with decaf.

Mattie noticed first and bit back a laugh. It took Jane a minute longer, but she looked as if she'd slept about as well as I had. I smiled again, merrily, and said, "Oh Jane. I have something for you."

I found my bag of energy drinks and handed her one. She looked confused, and I said, "I didn't sleep well and thought of you this morning. Maybe you need a little extra energy."

She smiled at me and admitted, "I am feeling worn down."

"Me too," I squeezed her shoulder and ignored Simon's silent protest. I crossed to the boxed cakes and pulled down the cake plates to fill them with last night's baking spree.

"Those look amazing," Mattie said, humor at Simon's rumbling carrying to me where I was working.

"Lemon chiffon and raspberry frosting," I said as I lifted the first cake and put up the pricing sign.

I added the carrot cake and chocolate cake and looked up to find Simon standing on the other side of the counter, watching me.

I grinned at him as if I didn't know he was irritated with my prank. The man did not like change. And I suspect he didn't like asparagus and sliced tomatoes. I had sprinkled them with balsamic vinegar and sea salt. If he'd given them a chance, he might have liked them.

"No Tara yet?"

I shook my head.

"You hear from her?"

I shook my head again. "She's usually not this late. But I heard that she and Kyle had been longtime friends."

Friends...or lovers...or enemies. They all seemed possible, but I wasn't going to add to whatever gossip Simon had been hearing about me and my staff. I also wasn't going to lie for the girl.

"When she comes in," he said, "would you please tell me?"

I nodded.

"Can I trust you to have Az make me a sandwich for lunch?"

My lips twitched, but I nodded.

"Tuna on rye," he said.

I called the order into Az.

"Maybe you could put a piece of cake in a box for me," he said. "Since you owe me one."

My laugh escaped then, but he didn't react at all. I pulled down the chocolate cake, not needing to hear what he wanted. The man needed to try new things. Given the flavor of the lemon chiffon cake, I suspected it was, by far, the best of the lot.

Az brought the order out. Given the way the bag bulged, I suspected Az was making his own apology for my prank. I added the cake and left Simon to Zee.

"Keep it up," Jane said as she paid Zee. "Simon needs a woman who doesn't cater to his every whim."

I handed Jane a slice of the lemon cake, all boxed up. "That was never going to be me."

"Thank you for what you did yesterday," she said.

I assumed she meant giving her the file Jenny had kept. I nodded once.

"It means a lot," she added.

Speaking of, I reminded myself silently, go to the hardware store and get new locks for the office and the closet off of the office. I nodded again then said brightly, "No worries."

I didn't want Zee to guess that Jane had a file in the office, that I'd given it to Jane, or to wonder what was inside. Jane lifted the cake slice then waved as she opened the door.

Mattie dropped cash on the table and ran from the restaurant, yelping, "I forgot my early appointment."

I waved at her and then glared at the single dirty table. I cleared it while Zee went about filling ketchup bottles. We worked in silence, waiting for Tara to show and wondering if Simon had found her. And hoping that more customers would arrive. The quiet was too intense and confirmed that all of us were worried.

I didn't want to believe that Tara could have had anything to do with Kyle's death. I far, far preferred to believe it was the girl with him —Morgan. Or some random passerby who'd come in for spaghetti and a little side of murder.

Not showing up, I reminded myself, was no reason to jump to murder. It only meant she was upset. And honestly, I wasn't surprised she was. They'd been on again off again since kindergarten. I'd have been upset too. Even if the last round of off again had ended with hatred and fury, he'd been her first love. She deserved to mourn him without serving coffee, and it wasn't like we needed the help.

✣ 13 ✣

"I'm going to run an errand," I told Zee as soon as we hit midmorning. We were always slow from 10:30 to around noon when people started coming in for lunch. Given how slow our morning had been, I was sure Zee and Az could cover anyone that came in.

I made my way to the car, bringing Daisy with me. She hopped into her spot in the front seat and I drove towards the edge of town, stopping at the feed store, which also had a hardware section. We restocked Daisy's food and snacks and then I went to talk to an employee about getting a set of locks and having them keyed to the same. I explained I was replacing an office lock and had to have someone walk me through what I would need to do to change it. After a few minutes of my blank looks—DIY was not something that was my strong suit or even the vaguest of interests—he offered to bring it to me and install it. That was a service I was happy to pay for, and I made my way to the customer service desk to set everything up.

The officer who'd responded to my car accident was also waiting.

"Hello," I greeted while Daisy sniffed his shoes.

He nodded at me once, and I knew that to him I was a murder

suspect. I picked up Daisy to hide my emotions, and asked, "How are you today?"

"Just fine, ma'am," he said.

I narrowed my eyes at being called ma'am, but I looked down at Daisy to hide my irritation. While I filled out the delivery form, I listened to the store manager talk about a recent robbery. My ears perked up at that. I thought this was a quiet beach town. Maybe I needed to re-key the entire diner. I had no idea who had keys. Suddenly, with the death of Kyle, doing anything less was stupid. I waited my turn, determined to have the entire diner updated. As I waited, I heard Roger, the store manager, state that he'd heard three other stores had been broken into recently.

"Yeah," the cop said. "That's true enough, Rog. But don't worry. The convenience store gets robbed often enough. The pharmacy had some unexpected things stolen—no actual cash. Probably happened when the store was open, and Pop's was robbed after closing time. They mostly took the petty cash and some steaks."

I pressed my lips together. We kept our cash in a floor safe, so we'd be okay as far as that went, but I was definitely, definitely updating our locks.

When the customer service person who was helping me came back, I said, "I heard you all had a robbery."

The older woman nodded. "Someone broke the glass and took a bunch of stuff. It was a mess. But no need to worry."

"You know," I said, "I think I'd be interested in updating all the locks at 2nd Chance Diner. Can you help me with that?"

She nodded, but she said, "Silver Falls is a good little town. With the robberies and that poor boy, I imagine you'd be concerned, but even with everything, I don't think there's any need to worry."

"So you don't think we killed him at 2nd Chance?"

The woman laughed, but she didn't sound too amused. "Any woman who would adopt and love that puppy, pay the boy for a free dog, keep Tara on, and put up with Zee and her mouth is not a killer."

The cop was clearly listening, and the store manager as well.

"It chaps my hide that you feel that way, sweet thing," the woman continued. "Zee speaks highly of you, and you know she doesn't speak highly of very many people. She was right worried when Jenny sold to you."

I realized that this woman was a friend of Zee's.

"What reason could you have to kill that boy? You or any of the folks over at 2nd Chance? People are *such idiots."* She worked as she raged, and I felt better with every passing moment of her tirade.

"It was one of his druggie friends. You wait and see. Like in some NCIS episode. That boy was killed because of his poor choices. His poor mother. You know Marilyn is a good woman. Those Johansson men are rough and tumble, but they're good men. She deserved to have her boy be like the men in her family. Good men. Not the mess he was."

I pressed my lips together before speaking. "Any death that young is a real tragedy. His poor mother."

I didn't know what else to say. I didn't know any of them and all I knew of Kyle was the sight of his dying face when I'd screamed for Jane, and the sight of him not facing me when he'd nearly killed Daisy and me.

"You're too right about a young man dying being a tragedy. Even if it's really for no one but his mom. You know she isn't seeing the idiot you met. She's seeing her baby. Her little boy. She's remembering Halloweens and Christmas mornings and the first day of school."

I felt sick at that.

"And, of course, remembering how she took care of him when he was sick and rocking him like mothers do. She's wishing for those simpler times back when he was only hers."

"Oh man," I said. "You sound like you know a little too much about loss like this."

"I've sat with more than one woman who's lost someone. I guess I can imagine it. My boys, praise God, are alive and well. One in Seattle. One in Portland. Five grandchildren. I'm a lucky woman."

I was both grateful that things had shifted to her and wishing for more gossip, but with our audience, I felt like perhaps it was better to move onto things like grandchildren.

"They sound lovely," I said, because what else could I say. She wasn't wearing a name tag, so I didn't even know her name. She was going to be the Feed Store Woman until I could put a name to her face.

"Well, dear, you are all set up. Now, don't you worry. These fools will find the killer," she said, nodding toward the cop, "and your life will be back to normal. We're right glad to have you here and to eat your good food. Your cakes have been the real highlight of my Friday afternoons."

Oh. She was the woman who joined Zee at the end of her shift. They cut a piece of cake and drank coffee together and stayed until after I'd mopped the floors and prepped for the next day. More than once, they'd been around when I'd started baking the cakes for the following day. I usually baked after closing time but before I went home for the day—only occasionally baking at the cottage like I had the night before.

I paid for my things and told the woman I was grateful for her help. They'd be sending someone out to the shop around 4:00 pm the next day, so that would have to be good enough.

WE CLOSED THE DINER WITHOUT TARA SHOWING UP. ZEE CROSSED the moment the closed sign flipped at 2:00 pm. "We have to figure this out. We barely made anything today. You're in the negative, sister."

She wasn't wrong. We'd spent a good amount of the day working on things that didn't need to be done. Every bit of the kitchen had been cleaned and restocked. I made cakes for the next day, and cookies and pancakes. We'd be donating most of the baked goods to the shelter in Lincoln City when they came by to pick up in the morning.

I glanced over at Zee and back at our empty diner. She was very right. I nodded to show my agreement. I wasn't too worried about one day's money, but without the inheritance money, days like this could kill a business. And of course, I wouldn't be successful in my dream if I couldn't make the diner profitable. First though, fix this mess. Then worry about profits.

I said, "We aren't going to recover until there's no question we didn't kill Kyle."

"You'd think they'd know better of us."

"They know better of you," I told her. Though to be honest if I were to imagine anyone as a killer, it would be Zee. But that was only imagination. I couldn't see it of any of us.

I glanced over at Zee and then back through the window to Az. He was a good man, and he'd worked hard to keep me happy today.

A part of me wanted to be like some horror movie female and wring my hands and demand for someone to help me. But I'd been a passenger in my own life and let myself be carried into the call center and only escaped after I'd been pushed far past my limits. I didn't want to be a passenger in my life anymore. I needed to take control of it, even if it was something like this, which I had no control over.

"What did Kyle's mom say?" I asked Zee.

"She doesn't think we killed him," Zee said sourly. "Everyone else there seemed to. But she knew better. She even worried about you. Said her boy owed you an apology and lied to her every morning about giving you one."

I sighed at the image of that. Kyle eating his Wheaties or whatever he'd had and experienced morning after morning of his mother asking him if he'd apologized to me. She'd been lied to every morning, so every morning known her son for what he was.

"I feel so bad for her," I said. She'd had the poor luck to have a son be partially lost to drugs, and she hadn't given up. I loved her for it.

"She's a good woman," Zee said, without any of her sourness. "With a real fondness for cake."

We all looked over at the untouched cakes. I'd cut exactly 3 pieces that day. One for Mattie, one for Jane, and one for Simon. Zee had a piece of the lemon for lunch, and Az had a smaller piece of each with his lunch.

"Do you think she'd be offended if we brought her the carrot cake?"

Zee shook her head. "Most of those folks work days. They won't show up to comfort her, not in full, until after closing time."

I glanced over at Az, who nodded once. The diner closed at 2:00 pm. We had about 3-4 hours before the folks who worked regular shifts were off.

I hated to do it. To show up at the mourning woman's house with cake and maybe learn a thing or two. But honestly, I would do it anyway. I would do it for me, and Tara, and Az, and Zee.

"What about Morgan?" Az asked as we carefully boxed up the carrot cake. "Someone needs to talk to her."

"We'll hit her next," Zee said. "And then we'll go after Tara."

I nodded and asked Az, "Would you keep Daisy? Can I come for her later?"

And talk to him without Zee around. I wanted to see if I could get him to spill his secret. I didn't want to believe he was the killer, and to be honest, I didn't want to believe any of us were but at different times, I could imagine all of us as the killer—myself included—and I knew I hadn't done it. It was crazy to be trying to find a killer. It wasn't like I had a forensics lab, but I did have ears and a mind and a willingness to ask questions.

🕱 14 🕱

Zee directed me to the Johansson house, and we walked up to the door together. Before Zee knocked, she glanced me over. "Remember we didn't kill Kyle and we don't have any guilt."

I realized that I had been feeling guilty. Would I have brought a cake to this woman if he'd died from drugs? Goodness, I hoped so. I decided in that moment to be the woman who heard of someone else's tragedy and reached out. I never wanted to feel guilty for bringing a cake again.

Zee knocked fiercely and, if you could declare it with a knock, with utter innocence.

The door was opened by a woman that I did not recognize.

"Hello Joyce," Zee greeted.

"Zee," she said. She glanced past Zee to me, her gaze fixated on the box, and then she opened the door slowly. "You've come again."

Zee stood there, without moving, and simply smiled.

Joyce eyed us both, considering. "I'll tell Margot you're here."

She let us in. "Just a second."

She held her hand out for the box, and I handed the cake over. We waited for a few minutes, and Zee sat down. She glanced up at me and hissed, "Being polite is leaving. Finding out what we need to know is sitting down."

I took a deep breath and crossed to the chair. As I looked around, I could see picture after picture of a boy who matched the features of the young man who'd nearly run me down. My sympathy was rising hard and fast, and I wanted to leave the woman be.

"Think of Tara," Zee whispered crossly. "And Az."

I crossed my hands in my lap, stiffening my spine, as a woman came into the room. A rush of sympathy was hitting me, and I wanted to run away and avoid this—except for Tara. Tara and Az and my dream.

"Hello, Margot," Zee said. She didn't adjust her tone from her normal tone. "This is Rosemary Baldwin. She was the one who called for Jane so quickly."

The woman nodded, her lips pressed together, and she sat down across from us. Goodness, I hated myself.

"Thank you for helping my baby," she said.

"I'm so sorry for your loss," I replied gently.

The woman nodded, nibbling at her lip.

"Rose made you a cake," Zee lied. "It's carrot cake. We hope you like it."

"Thank you," she said. She sniffled. "I'm sorry. It's been a hard day."

"Please don't apologize," I begged. I reached out and took her hand without thinking, but her fingers dug into mine as if she had been waiting for someone to let her know she wasn't alone.

"Margot," Zee said carefully. "I have been so bothered since I found out about Kyle. Is anyone in your family diabetic?"

She looked up and she wasn't thinking clearly enough to realize what Zee was doing or to see her heavy-handed lie. "Oh no. We're all healthy. Like horses."

She sounded like she wasn't registering what we were saying. I scooted closer to her, wrapping my arm around her and tucking her into my body. I wasn't her friend. I didn't know anything about her, but she sank into me.

"Was he depressed?" Zee asked as I rubbed Margot's shoulder.

"Oh no. He never was, you know," she said, choking on her words. "He was so angry. Angry at everyone. He couldn't say anything nice ever. He was mean to Morgan. Awful to Tara. He was terrible to every-one. How could I be a little relieved?"

She wailed, and I clutched her tighter, cooing to her.

"You aren't yourself," Zee said flatly. "Your mind is racing and not at anchor. You don't feel that way. Not really."

Margot shuddered in my arms, but she was shaking her head slightly against my shoulder. "He was such wonderful baby. But by school, he was always in trouble."

I hugged her even closer.

"No one you know is diabetic?" Zee asked. She was maybe a little gentler, but her voice was firm. I wouldn't have been surprised to hear her tell a dog to sit in the same tone of voice.

"My mother, but she's in Kansas," Margot said, holding in tears.

"But no one you know in Silver Falls is diabetic."

She pulled away from me for a moment and frowned at Zee in confusion. I was starting to suspect that Margot was on some sort of valium or calming pill. She was too compliant.

She shook her head. "No...no...I don't think so."

"There's Martha Pickerson, of course," said the woman who'd opened the door. She crossed into the living room and handed Margot a piece of the carrot cake. "And Glory Bean. And Kiera Markowitz, and Gus Longfellow. Look dear, it's your favorite."

"Oh..." Margot blinked down at the cake. "I couldn't."

"Come now," Joyce said, "You don't want to make Zee and Rose sad. They worked so hard on this cake for you. And you haven't eaten nearly enough."

I rose as Joyce bullied Margot into eating cake and examined the pictures. There were several pictures of Kyle, of course, and of another boy. I assume the second boy was a brother or cousin. Someone Margot loved as much as Kyle. I hoped. I hoped she had another son. There was even a picture of Tara and Kyle and one of Tara, Kyle, and Morgan. There were also several of Margot's spouse including one outside of the cannery. What gave me pause was the sight of Eddie in those cannery coveralls.

❧ 15 ❧

"**G**lory Bean? As in Tara Bean? Our Tara?"

"Tara's grandmother," Zee snapped. She sounded furious. She slammed the car door and crossed her arms over her chest. "Drive towards your place."

I looked at her before starting the car. The Johansson's only lived a few blocks from Main Street, and I wasn't too far from it. I turned down on Nehalem Road towards the ocean. The cottage I was staying in was at the very end of Nehalem, but there were about a half-dozen side streets before Nehalem ended at the ocean. Zee directed me to turn down the second one and had me park at the cross-section. The house was on the corner of the two roads and it sparked a memory in me. This was where I'd heard people arguing the first day I'd been in Silver Falls. I had seen Tara leave this house in a rage.

There was a line of dogwoods in front of the house, and I had stood underneath one of them when the girl had come stomping out of the house after screaming. I examined the house closely and found a charming yellow, wood house with white shutters and a white porch. The grass was a swathe of green and the flower beds were a profusion of late-planted petunia and bachelor's buttons.

Goodness, I hoped that Tara wasn't the killer. A sick feeling was forming in my stomach, and I couldn't get out of the car.

"Don't be a wuss," Zee snarled opening the door and slamming it.

When I didn't immediately follow, she leaned down and gave me a sour look. I took a long slow breath, told myself that finding the killer was the right thing to do, and followed Zee up the little cement path.

Zee rang the doorbell ferociously, and I waited behind her, not wanting to be held responsible for the way Zee jabbed that buzzer.

The door opened and a woman who had to be near Zee's age stared out at us. The woman must have been Glory, Tara's grandmother. She was near Zee's size both in height and thinness, but her hair was cut in a diagonal style and looked to have been highlighted with shades of gray.

She frowned. "I should have guessed it would be you."

I paused at that, but the woman expanded, "Only Zapphirah Snow would ring the doorbell as if she were being chased by a band of pirates."

"Get with the times, Glory. Zombies. Surely you watch *The Walking Dead*."

The woman opened the door. "Gives me nightmares. And it's gross."

"I'm surrounded by wilting flowers today. Both of you need to get a spine." Zee barged past Glory and made herself comfortable on the sofa in the living room.

"Why are you here?" Glory asked, following more slowly, she gave me a curious glance but directed herself to Zee.

"This is Rose. She bought Jenny's."

I prevented myself from saying 2nd Chance. Now wasn't the time. Instead, I followed Zee into the living room. The couches were worn, and glass fishing floats were set here and there with seeming reckless-ness, but it all came together to make a homey, deliberate picture. There was nothing pretentious about Glory Bean's house, despite its utter loveliness.

Glory had been sitting in the living room and her armchair had a phone plugged into a little speaker. It was playing music quietly next to where a book was laying open over the arm of the chair. I caught the picture of a teacup and was able to read the title, *Hot Tea & Cold Murder*. My interest was piqued, but I knew I'd have to save looking up the book until after the investigation was over. And probably after I'd stress-baked several layer cakes.

"And why are *you* and Tara's boss coming to my house?"

"You missing insulin? When did you become diabetic anyway?"

Glory's eyes narrowed. She and Zee stared each other down without either of them twitching a muscle. There was something about the way they faced off that said it wasn't the first time.

"I might be old," Glory said, "but I am not stupid. And none of your business."

"You're not old," Zee countered. "Because then I would be old. And I'm as sprightly as ever."

"That's your sourness. Everyone else is feeling their age."

"Um," I said, trying to calm the two women who seemed to have a long trail of ugliness behind them. "Maybe—"

"As it happens," Glory cut in with a snap to her voice, "I am *not* missing any insulin."

"You lyin'?" Zee leaned back and crossed her bony leg over her knee.

I pressed my lips together. She had given me the nastiest look, and I had to interpret it as Zee knowing what she was doing.

"I am not," Glory said. "How dare you come into my house and—"

"Please," Zee cut in. "We've known each other long enough for you to know better."

Glory leaned back and crossed her fingers over her chest. She eyed us both carefully. "What's your aim here?"

"The diner was dead today. It's never dead. That second-rate coffee joint across the street was hopping with people actually standing outside to wait to get in. *Our* regulars."

"Cry me a river," Glory said. She gave Zee a little smirk before glancing at me. "Sorry."

She wasn't, of course. She'd have been absolutely fine with me losing the diner if it made Zee upset.

"I don't understand," I said, glancing between the two of them. Neither of them looked at me, and it couldn't have been more evident that they didn't care what I didn't understand. But how could they both love Tara so much and still hate each other like this?

"This ridiculous town thinks one of us killed Kyle," Zee said. "Maybe they're focused on Rose right now, but you and I both know that's stupid thinking, and pretty soon they'll start wondering about the rest of us."

"So you want to clear your name?"

"*All* of our names," Zee said. "Including Tara's name. I *would* say, can you believe the fools in this town? But who's surprised."

Glory hummed in the back of her throat. "I wouldn't help you catch Tara. You're here because you think she could have taken my insulin and killed that idiot."

"Do you think it's possible Tara—" I couldn't even finish. I knew my eyes were wide and that I hadn't hidden the shock. It didn't matter. Those two old broads were focused on each other to the exclusion of me.

"Tara loves hard," Glory said. She left it at that, and I wasn't sure how to interpret something so vague.

Zee cleared her throat. "We're trying to clear *all* of our names. We aren't here because we suspect Tara. We're here because—"

"Because I'm diabetic, I have insulin, and you think my grandbaby could have killed that..." The distaste in her voice let me know exactly what she thought of Kyle Johansson.

Zee stared at Glory, and I decided to follow Zee's example and wait.

"It just so happens," Glory said slowly, "that I am not missing any insulin."

Zee uncrossed her legs. "Excellent."

"Not so quick," Glory said. "I did, however, have to wait to get my prescription when I went to refill it last week. There was a snafu about their stock."

Zee leaned back in her chair. The venom had left Glory's voice and the two women seemed to come to an unspoken truce.

"I ended up waiting far longer than usual," Glory added. "Turns out that when the pharmacy was broken into a whole mess of drugs was taken, including insulin. Weird stuff. Antibiotics. Prenatal vitamins. Tylenol. A bunch of other things. The pharmacist—always a bit slow—was befuddled and bemoaning his fate. It took him a while to get me what I needed, and he kept muttering about needing to get more in right away."

"Insulin?"

"Amongst other things." Glory said with a sideways look at Zee.

"Like drugs that users want? Maybe like Kyle?"

Glory started to nod. "That I don't know. I only overhead some of it. They saw me listening." That sourness in her voice was back.

"Would you kill someone using insulin?" Zee asked.

"Do you want to know if I knew how? Of course I do. But did I?" Glory shrugged. "I wanted to get rid of that stupid boy since Tara was in 2nd grade, but I didn't kill him. I wish I had, in a lot of ways. Way back then. If I'd know what was coming, I might have."

I could hardly believe my ears. I mean, what did she know? I thought about the time my heart had been broken and how I'd cried in my mom's arms. What if Glory had been the one to hold Tara time and again?

"She wanted him back so bad, you know?" Glory reached out and took Zee's hand. "How did she become so willing to accept how he treated her?"

"You know how," Zee said gently. She squeezed Glory's hand. The two of them looked at each other, remembering things I'd never know.

"Oh, I see," I said suddenly, glancing between the two of them.

"See what?" The two of them faced me as one, heads tilted to the same angle, eyes squinted in the same manner.

"You two..." I shook my head. Peas in a pod. Old friends. Old enemies. Given the daggers they were throwing at me with their eyes, I stood. "If you aren't going to confess or tell us how Tara couldn't have done it, I have errands to run."

Zee looked at me, but she was only a few blocks from the diner. She was more than capable of walking to where her car was parked or she could get Glory to provide a ride.

"It was nice meeting you, Glory," I said. "I'm sorry it wasn't under better circumstances."

I escaped before they started throwing actual daggers at each other or, for that matter, me. I suspected that they'd fought over a man once —like some sort of 1960s comedy heroine. Or perhaps one of them had been the queen of the prom or squash queen or something and the other had been the very, very unhappy runner-up. Maybe they'd once been best friends and had a falling out.

I got into the car, glanced at where Daisy should be sitting and wondered if I should get her first. Maybe I'd head to the pharmacy? I was pretty sure it was at the end of the main street through Silver Falls. I needed a break, though, to clear my head. Right then, I wasn't sure if I suspected Eddie, Az, or Tara more, but I hated that I suspected all of them.

Silver Falls was named after a waterfall that poured into the ocean. It was gorgeous, and I hadn't been to see it since I bought the diner. Instead of going on with the investigation or the things I should do, I went to the state park and parked in the lot. It was deserted and wet and my shoes would be coated in mud, but I started the short climb to the falls anyway. When I reached the edge where the falls poured over the cliffs down into the ocean, I sat on the stone bench and closed my eyes.

What was it, I wondered, about the scent of water in the air? Salty sea air, rain, or this waterfall left me feeling so willing to do strange and wonderful things. I had quit a steady job without a parachute. Sure, I'd inherited money, but I had never expected that. I'd decided to investigate a murder which was not my responsibility and when I knew they'd never find evidence to falsely convict me. Sure, it would have been uncomfortable for a few days, but once the killer was caught, the diner would have gotten busy again. And yet, even as I took a break at the waterfall, ready to swig my next 5-hour energy drink, I knew I'd make my way to the pharmacy to see what I could find out, and then to Az to get Daisy and ask him about his brother and the lies. Maybe even about the lack of the file.

I shook my head and took a long breath. It was cold and my jacket was not enough for the Oregon Coast wind, but regardless I sat in the cold and let the peace of the ocean fill me. I wasn't sure how this had become my life—I had envisioned something so much more cozy and sweet. It had come, though, and as much as I'd like to step aside, I knew I would not.

I finally rose and walked back to my car. I pulled out my phone and texted my mom long paragraphs of what I had on my mind and what was happening. I'm sure it would be a surprising jumble when she got it, but I wasn't too worried. I just didn't want to have to explain later why I hadn't told her.

As soon as I sent the final bit of the story, I drove my way towards town again, looking at each place, each passing moment afresh, new and beloved. In a lot of ways, it felt like fate had brought me here, and I was grateful for it, no matter how different than I'd expected.

I went inside the diner, locking the door behind me, and walked down the long counter, admiring the glass display where I put baked goods. On the top of that were my funky cake plates. I only had three so far, but I wanted to have enough for pies and piles of Christmas cookies before the holidays. I took a moment to enjoy my cake plates, the dark wood floors, and the new, deep plum vinyl on the benches. The 2nd Chance Diner was starting to become a reality of what I had sketched in my journal.

❧ 16 ❧

I walked through the kitchen to the row of lockers near the rear door. This was where we brought in deliveries and kept our shelves of food. The employee bathroom was back here, along with a small room full of things I hadn't had time to go through. There was an employee only sign on the other side of one door and you could access the area through that door and through the kitchen.

I opened the first locker and found some things that clearly belonged to Az. I shuffled through them, but it was an extra sweater, a knit cap, an extra set of keys, a picture of a woman that I hadn't met, and another of his family. I closed it. Nothing there.

The next locker was empty. The one after that was Zee's. It had pictures of cats on the inside, a couple of bucktoothed little kids I hadn't met, hair spray, and deodorant. It was stocked with anything she might need, but none of it was suspicious.

The next locker was Tara's. She had random things like hairspray and an extra protein bar. I found a bottle of prenatal vitamins and remembered her saying something about trying to grow her nails longer. She had a note taped inside the door in handwriting I recognized as Jenny's, reading, 'Don't Be Late Tomorrow!' If I had expected a glaring sign of guilt, I didn't find it. I sighed, feeling like quite the jerk for going through their things. I went back to my office and looked at the mess I'd made going through the files. I just didn't want to believe that any of them could be responsible for what had happened.

Given the way that everyone had talked about Kyle, he wasn't well liked. In fact, as far as I could tell, *only* Morgan and Tara might even mourn the kid. Of course, his mother and his family were upset, but they were aware of what their loved one had been and their mourning was tinged by the fact that he'd made their lives so difficult.

I walked out of the diner by the back door with that terrible thought. I was certain, if I died, my mom would be devastated. Margot's sorrow seemed tinged by how often Kyle had devastated her while he was alive.

The pharmacy was about four blocks away on the other end of the downtown area, past the restaurants and touristy little shops. I walked to it, noticing two people actually cross the street to avoid me. Did they really think *I* was the killer? Maybe I was only reading into their movements. I passed the town hall and saw Roberta in the daylight in her office. She eyed me like I was trash, and I hoped that was the reason people were avoiding me. I nodded at her, though I had to force myself to, and crossed the street to go into the pharmacy.

It wasn't busy inside, but the guy behind the counter still seemed stressed.

I smiled at him. "Hello."

He nodded, then leaned down to pick up a box and carry it to an aisle near the registers. As he was shelving items, I grabbed a basket and decided to wander a bit, checking the place out. After a few minutes of grabbing random things, I had to laugh at myself. I had liquid eyeliner, mascara, Pringles, and four bags of fun-sized chocolates.

I made my way over to the guy, who was frantically stocking the shelves, and cleared my throat.

"Can I help you?"

He did not want to help me.

I refrained from smiling again, since I intended to have a series discussion. "I heard you guys were broke into. I was thinking of transferring my prescriptions, but I don't want to do that if it's not safe."

What crap, I thought, but I glanced around as if I were nervous and waiting for someone to jump out from behind the chips.

"You don't need to worry about that," he assured me. "They already fired the girl who was involved."

"It was a staff person?" *Who,* I wanted to demand, but I waited.

He stood up. "She was around when a lot of the thefts happened. Even if she didn't do it, she probably knows who did. And the management isn't happy about cans of formula, prescription drugs, and cash being stolen. There hasn't been a problem since she got fired."

"Who got fired?" I tried to ask it without sounding like I was fishing for gossip.

He frowned at me, hesitating. "Morgan Brown," he finally answered as though confirming rumors. "They didn't prove it was her, though. You know? You can't say she was a thief," he said as if he had second thoughts about talking to me.

I smiled sweetly, "Oh, I won't."

I paid for my things and left the pharmacy to find Simon waiting outside, leaning against his truck.

"What are you doing in there, Rosemary?" He asked it in a way that said he might have a pretty good idea.

I held up my bag and pulled out the can of Pringles, popping it open and taking a few. I offered them to him.

He shook his head. "You passed a convenience store to get those?"

"I got eyeliner, too," I said brightly.

"Rose..."

I smiled and started walking back to my diner. He followed and that made me smile a little wider.

"So Morgan Brown stole insulin from the pharmacy?"

"Rose..."

"Always the third wheel," I said. "Never the partner."

"Rose..."

I turned and walked backward to face him.

"Rose," he said quietly. "*What* are you doing?"

"Gossiping. How did you know I was gossiping?"

"Glory," he said. "She doesn't like Zee very much."

I'd noticed. "Did Zee steal her boyfriend? Back in the day?"

"Last year," Simon said.

"Shut the front door," I gasped and then laughed.

"Before that, they were very close. It has caused quite a division in the knitting circle and ladies auxiliary society."

My laughter morphed into giggles. I had to stop walking, especially backward, and glanced at the building we were standing by. It was an ice cream parlor and suddenly, I just *needed* ice cream therapy. I walked inside, letting him come or go as he wanted.

I went with a double scoop of Tillamook mountain blackberry and white chocolate raspberry. Yum. I got them in a waffle bowl with a spoon. Simon ordered straight vanilla. Oh, the poor man, I thought. I was going to torture him with flavors as soon as this mess was cleared up.

"What are you up to?" he asked as we left the shop.

"It's all Zee," I tried.

"But you went to Zee's house, not the other way around."

"Who me?" I took a bite of my ice cream and looked up at him.

He considered my innocent expression for a moment, but before he could ask me more questions, I asked, "No coconut?"

I watched him sort of squirm and I added, "Chocolate chips? Walnuts? Cookies? Peanut butter?"

I didn't want a specific answer, because I had every intention of baking something detailed and full of coconut just to watch him choke it down.

"I like vanilla," he said simply, taking a bite of his ice cream. "What are you up to with Zee?"

"Mostly listening to her harass people I've never met before," I said.

Okay, someone's head definitely turned and watched us as we walked down the street. What were they thinking? That Simon was questioning me again? He was. Or perhaps they were thinking we were walking down the street together as friends, maybe something more. We had done that before. It wasn't so outlandish.

"I need you to stop," he said.

"Have you talked to Tara?"

He shook his head at me and then chucked his ice cream into the trash. Mine was therapy and it wasn't going anywhere except down the hatch.

Rather than taking him into the diner, I plopped onto the bench outside and took another bite of my ice cream. Tillamook really did make excellent ice cream. It made me want to road trip up to the factory and get a bunch of their different, fun cheeses.

"I need you to stop interfering, Rose," he said, standing over me.

"She didn't show for work," I said. I had to crane my head to look up at him. "We're worried about her."

"I need you to *stop*," he repeated.

I took another bite and looked him over. He was earnest. I knew he wanted what was best for me, maybe for all of us, but I also knew I wasn't sure I could feel good about myself if I didn't check up on Az and Tara. Maybe after that I could let it go. I wouldn't even know what to do after talking to them now that Morgan seemed to be the likeliest suspect, but I wasn't going to make any promises.

"You heard about the insulin being stolen from the pharmacy?" I asked, taking another bite. I knew he had.

He sat next to me, and the look he gave me was a little disgusted.

"I wouldn't have suspected that you'd be so stubborn. Or so prone to butting in."

"You can't honestly expect me to just *hope* that you'd know about the insulin?"

"Of *course* I know it," he snapped. He folded his arms over his chest and leaned back. We both stopped speaking as Paige from the boutique crossed behind us. If she had to go that way, right then, I'd eat my shoes. She didn't usually have help during the day, which meant she'd left her shop closed to make that trek. Yeah. Right.

"Morgan hasn't come back from Seaside," Simon said. "She'll be back soon, and we'll talk to her."

"She doesn't answer the phone?"

"She didn't take a charger," he said.

I looked at him until he looked away. I didn't believe that. He surely didn't. Even if she hadn't, she'd have bought or borrowed one. Pretty much everyone used a mini USB or an apple charger.

"Interesting how both Tara and Morgan are gone right now."

"Interesting," he said. "I'm not doing this with you, Rose. No matter how much I like you."

I had to hide my smile by taking another bite of ice cream. I might become forever fond of these two flavors of ice cream just because he'd admitted he felt *something* for me. He might be handsome and kind, but he moved as quickly as an old man, and he was as stubborn as an oak tree.

"Stay out of it, please," he said and then stopped what would no doubt have been a continued lecture because his phone was buzzing. Whatever he saw on the screen had him standing up immediately. He touched my shoulder for a moment. "See you later."

I tried not to read too much into the fact that he'd given me that moment to say goodbye rather than just dashing off. I also tried not to wish I'd gotten a look at his phone's screen. Instead, I sat in the cool sunshine, ate my ice cream, and planned. I was going to need a hot coffee after this, but bringing two to Az's place to get Daisy would give him a reason to invite me to stay, and me a reason to ask him what was going on with him and his brother.

I considered for a moment and then messaged Zee that Simon had hurried off with whatever he'd been told. I couldn't do anything with that information, but Zee could.

17

Before I drove to Az's, I downed another 5-hour energy and went back to my cottage to take a few minutes to gather my thoughts. I called my mom and she scolded me about letting the murder investigation get me down, telling me it was just bad luck. I let her counsel me until she needed to leave for her *date*. I tried not to be jealous, but I wanted to be getting ready for a date rather than preparing to go get my dog, harass my favorite employee, and then go home to crash after my third 5-hour energy wore off.

I drove to Az's and parked outside. When I walked up to his door, I carried the two to-go coffee cups. When he opened the door, he looked behind him before speaking. "Oh, hey."

He stepped out, called for Daisy, and closed the door. I stared at him and then at the door as Daisy leaped around my legs.

"Um," he said.

I narrowed my eyes and handed him the coffees to pick up Daisy and say hello. Once I set her down, I asked, "You hiding your brother in there?"

"What? No." He was so startled that I believed him, but I was sure he was hiding something. Or someone.

My head cocked and I sidestepped him. Before he could stop me, I opened the door. Tara was curled up on the couch, crying. She didn't look up, and I didn't say anything. Instead, I quietly closed the door before she noticed me.

"Oh goodness," I said, taking a deep breath. I looked up at him and raised my brows.

"She was here when I got home," he said finally and very simply. "She knows where Eddie and I keep our extra key. I guess she just needed someplace to be alone. Her mom and grandmother are prone to lecturing the girl. Y'know?"

I nodded, believing him. I'd seem him text Tara when Zee and I had been calling. We, all of us, had been worried.

Just because I believed, though, didn't mean I had forgotten I had other questions. I glanced around. Az and Eddie lived in a little, single-wide trailer on a piece of land near the mountains. I wasn't entirely sure it was a real address or was on someone else's property. I did pass a rather large farmhouse up the road to get to this little thing.

"Did you know about the files that Jenny kept?"

He froze, then slowly nodded.

"Did you take yours?"

If possible, he became even more still. "I wasn't aware it was missing."

I examined his face and thought that I believed him. He looked shaken enough. I hoped I wasn't being foolish. But unless Zee took it, Jenny had. Why had Jenny taken *only* Az's file?

On that thought, I pulled out my phone and texted Zee that Tara and I were at Az's. I bet she would come, and she might admit she'd taken the file when she realized I was pushing Az about it.

"Why did Jenny protect *only* you?"

He frowned. "I don't know."

I had worked with him for hours, and we'd chatted a lot. I thought I knew him, but I was surprised to find how well I could read him. Or perhaps he was only a bad liar and I was only now noticing.

"You do too," I pressed.

He didn't answer. He didn't look away, though, either.

I took my coffee back from him and took a sip. I was stalling until Zee arrived. I had *no* intention of leaving until we talked to Tara, and I was sure she'd lie right to my face. Zee, however, knew Tara enough to know when she was lying or not.

As for Az, he didn't need to know I was drinking coffee to slow down his getting rid of me.

"Why don't you try telling me?"

"It doesn't affect only me."

There was a little fire pit with old folding chairs around it, and I crossed and sat down, putting my feet up on one of the rocks that formed the fire pit. Daisy jumped onto my lap. Az sat down with me reluctantly. It was quiet for a while, and I tried to add up what I was seeing about Az's life.

I knew what Jenny had paid, and what I still paid, Az for his job at the diner. With a factory income from Eddie, surely they could do better than this place? I doubted the two brothers paid more than $500 a month, probably in rent and not mortgage. It was as nice as they could make it, but there was no denying it was a rundown old place they lived in.

Suddenly it all clicked together.

"You're illegal," I said.

He started, but he finally spoke. "Eddie is. I married an American girl when I was young. And I came over not long after." He relaxed when I didn't comment. "I didn't want to go back. If I were legal, we'd have broken up within months, but she was kind. She lived a sham with me for years so I could stay and become a citizen."

"Az..." I wanted to shake him. Why hadn't he said something? "It's why Eddie left on his pretend fishing trip. It's why you lied about where he was. You guys were hiding who you were."

"I don't really hide," Az defended. "I live here because I want to. I cook because I want to. I could get another job. But Eddie...he came to visit about two years after I was legal, and he never left. I told him to. I tried. He should have. He's been here so long, though. He'll get banned for staying."

I reached out. "I'll help you get an immigration lawyer."

He laughed at me. "It's not easy, Rose. Eddie—"

"What about to Canada? It's nearby. You could see each other often. I could help with that. We could find a Canadian lawyer and see what could be done. I'll help you, however I can. But first, I think we need to help Tara."

"You think she killed Kyle?"

I rubbed my forehead. "I think it was Tara or Morgan, and I very, very much want it to be Morgan."

Az paled. I followed his gaze towards the long gravel drive. It was Zee's car followed by Simon's truck.

"Oh," I said. I hadn't realized that in telling Zee, I'd be telling Simon. But if Tara hadn't killed Kyle, she could trust Simon. She could trust him to help her as much as he could, regardless. If Tara had killed Kyle—

I didn't want to think about it.

"Shall we do this?" Az asked. He stood and held a hand for me.

"Is Eddie gone?"

"He is. If this all gets cleared up, there won't be any reason for anyone to know he did anything other than go for a quick fishing trip."

I squeezed his hand. "I'll do what I can."

"Why would you help us, Rose?"

"I like you," I told him. "And people should help each other and be kind."

"You don't think he should be kicked out of the country?"

"I think lives are complicated and messy."

"He's my only family left," Az said. "After Jen and I broke up, he came over because I realized how much I loved her and she was over me. She was over me and beyond me, and I was falling apart. He came to put me back together, and I wasn't back together by the time his Visa was up."

My heart was breaking for these brothers. "I wish I could fix it."

"Me too," he said, sounding so very tired. "We didn't do any of the things we should have and now we're in this mess. We were *so* stupid."

"We'll do what we can," I said again, hoping that there was *something* that could be done.

❧ 18 ❧

Zee got out of the car, her face stiff. For the first time since I had met her, Zee looked old. I wondered if that meant Tara had killed Kyle. My heart froze at the thought. She was only a kid. A good one. She wasn't a drug-using jerk. She worked hard, she was quiet, but what had Tara's grandmother said? Tara loved hard.

A part of me was jealous of the mere idea of loving hard. I wanted to have something more to my life even though I was loving the life I'd created. I had messed up with Simon, and I needed to apologize.

Simon got out of his truck. His gaze met mine. This wasn't the place or the time, but I tried to make my face look as sorry as I actually felt. I just hadn't known exactly how sorry I'd be until I saw how his gaze fixed on mine and how his eyes had slid past me as if he had something to hide.

I hadn't known Tara was here when I'd come to get Daisy. And yet, I'd texted Zee, not Simon. He didn't look pleased, but he didn't say anything. Which meant he didn't make me leave.

Zee went into the trailer. Simon followed. Should I ask permission to stay? I took breath, looked at Az, and we followed them.

Zee had stopped in the living room and was staring at Tara, who hadn't moved from her fetal position, curled facing the back of the couch.

"Have you figured out what happened yet?" I whispered to Zee. She shook her head and turned to Az.

"Water. And coffee."

Zee crossed to the sofa, picked up a chair, and set it near the side of the couch where Tara's head was.

"Hey," Zee said with a gentleness I hadn't known she was capable of. When Tara turned towards them, I had to wince at the look on her face. It was *terrible*.

"I..." Tara dropped her head back to her arms and snuggled her face in.

Az came back, handing over the drinks before he took a seat in the corner.

Zee's head cocked. "Up, girl."

There was something in her tone that got Tara sitting up and facing us.

"Tell us," Zee said.

I looked at Tara, noticed the way her hands were shaking, the way she seemed so very, very sad. She looked like she'd been through something terrible. Was this what it was like to lose your longtime boyfriend? I suddenly wasn't so sure I wanted to love that hard.

I took a deep breath and crossed to sit near Tara's feet. She looked ill now. I remembered that I'd noticed black circles under her eyes for weeks.

"It's more than Kyle, isn't it?" I asked gently.

Tara looked at me, blinking slowly.

"It has to be more than that," I said. "You have been off for a while. Haven't you? I don't think I knew you before you were like this. But she's different isn't she?" I asked the others.

Az choked and cleared his throat. "She has been off for a while. Little love...won't you trust us?"

"I'm not blind," Tara said. She took the coffee between shaking hands. "That's Simon over there. He's a cop."

"I'm not your enemy, Tara," Simon told her, stepping forward.

Tara shook her head. "Yeah. I'm my own enemy. That's what my

grandma says. Since I've been little. I always thought she was old-fash-
ioned and uptight."

"Does she know why you're so upset?"

"Parts of it," Tara said.

"What did she tell you to do?" Zee asked, pushing back Tara's
hair.

"She told me to be my own person. To make my own fate."

"And how are you supposed to do that?"

"I already ruined everything." She smiled weakly at Zee. "Why do
you care what Grandma said? You two hate each other."

"We've hated each other many times over the years," Zee said,
squeezing Tara's hand. "It gives our lives spice."

"How did you ruin everything?" I asked. "Your Grandma didn't
want you to go back to Kyle. She didn't want you to be with him. Did
she want you to leave Silver Falls?"

Tara shook her head. "No. She wanted me to do what the women in
our family do. Generation after generation after generation."

Zee stiffened. "Are you saying…"

Tara's eyes filled with tears. "Not anymore."

It was the way she said it, the way she curled around herself, the
way she triggered a thousand little memories and one recent one. Of
the locker. Of the prenatal vitamins. Of the way she'd never spoken of
a father. Of the way her grandmother's walls were covered with
pictures of them. Of the possibility of what that life the generations of
the Bean women lived. "You…you were pregnant."

Her lips trembled. "I wanted my baby. But Kyle—" Her voice
caught.

I looked over at Simon and it was suddenly all coming together.

"Kyle didn't."

Tara nodded, her lips still trembling.

"Would it have complicated things with Morgan?"

"You have *no* idea," Tara said. "Morgan… I didn't have any idea.
How could she?"

"She was your best friend. And she weaseled her way into something with Kyle?"

"Her family, they're not rich. But for Silver Falls, they *are* better off.

We're just the Bean women with our little house and our second-rate jobs."

The disgust in Tara's voice did not nearly match the disgust I felt. That kid...that stupid, stupid kid, Kyle. I knew he had been selfish, but I'd like to kill him for the way he'd broken Tara. Only, she'd been broken for a while, and we'd all missed it.

"Oh, Tara, honey," Zee said in the same loving, kind voice that I doubted more than a half-dozen people had heard from her.

My mind was racing a thousand miles an hour. "You didn't break into the pharmacy or the feed store or any of the other places. That was Kyle and Morgan."

"The Beans are endlessly honest," Zee said.

I could tell by the look on Tara's face that she hadn't been the one who had broken in. And yet, the memory of the things that had been stolen kept hold of me.

"You said Kyle and Morgan were whispering together that night at the diner, Zee," I said to her.

Zee nodded, her gaze examining mine.

"I—" I didn't want to say what I was thinking. I didn't want it to be true. I met Tara's gaze, and she knew that I knew. She nodded once.

"Morgan is pregnant too." I spoke the news for her. "You were both pregnant at the same time. He convinced *you* to abort the baby because he would have been worthless to Morgan's family if you both came up pregnant. He'd never have been able to slide his way through that one. Never. He'd have always been a deadbeat."

Tara nodded, trembling, and a tear rolled down her face.

"You didn't know about Morgan's baby. He promised you something?"

"We'd go away," Tara said. "We'd start again. Somewhere else. He'd stop using."

"So you did it," I said. "And then you came home from going through it all by yourself, and he—"

"He was in bed with Morgan," Tara replied.

Zee snarled under her breath, and Az rose and punched the wall. I didn't want to finish, but Tara nodded at me. The gesture motioned me to continue.

I pressed my hand to my mouth, wanting to hold it back but knowing that was wrong, too. Simon might not have proof yet, but he would. I thought he'd do what he could to help her, but he had to have reason. Proof of her remorse for what she'd been driven to. I hoped. And I recalled the promise I'd made to Az—I'd do what I could for her.

"But you found out Morgan was pregnant that night. You somehow got the insulin they stole from the pharmacy. Probably mistakenly. But you what, put it in the drinks? Making sure Kyle got the poisoned one."

"Morgan only drinks unsweetened ice tea," Tara said, and Zee closed her eyes. "I didn't know she was pregnant. Not until I heard them whispering in the corner, waiting for their booth. I saw her mouth. I saw her hold her stomach. I just knew. I'd had an abortion I didn't want because of his promises. I should have known better."

Her self-hate made me even sadder. There wasn't enough ice cream therapy for these revelations. I crossed my arms over my stomach to hold in the pain I felt for her. She finished for me, which was good because I didn't want to ask any more questions.

"I took a bunch of the stuff they stole when I found them together. I was going to turn them in. I was going to hand over the proof, but later I realized it would be their word against mine. They'd have ganged up and lied. They did in 3rd grade. They'd do it again."

I let the history I didn't know as the new girl in town go, and I looked at her. I *wanted* to save her, to make it better. I glanced at Simon and pled, "Isn't there anything we can do?"

He took a breath. "I'll do everything I can."

"It's not her fault. I'd be wringing his neck right now if he were in front of me. You'd have had to pull me off his carcass," Zee said. She stood and punched the wall right next to where Az was. I looked over and saw they both had tears in their eyes. This was *our* Tara. She'd been so wronged, and we'd help catch her.

"Thank you," Tara said. "Thank you. I knew I had to say something, but I didn't know how." She stood. "I guess this is it, huh?"

I was crying, so I couldn't see her face clearly, but I crossed to her, holding her as tightly as I could and whispered, "I'll do what I can."

"Okay," she said, but she squeezed me back.

Zee hugged her next and Tara said, "Take care of Mom and Grandma for me, please."

Zee nodded into the girl's hair, kissing her on both cheeks. "You're *not* alone."

Az didn't say anything, but he hugged her so hard that he lifted her off the ground. After he released her, he slammed his fist into the wall of the trailer again, adding a third hole and bloodying his knuckles.

Simon took Tara gently by the arm, and they walked out of the trailer together with the three of us left watching them go.

"Damn it," I said. "Damn it."

Zee swallowed hard. "Wine." Her voice broke.

"I've only got whiskey," Az told her.

"That'll do."

🧩 19 🧩

It took three days for us to gain the heart to re-open the diner. Zee kicked Az and me into it, and when we were serving only pancakes, no one minded. They wanted the gossip. I let Zee and Az serve every table and spent my morning flipping pancake after pancake. There was something so soothing in the monotony.

"Why don't you guys serve a normal menu?"

I glanced over and saw an old man standing near the window.

"We just lost someone. We're gathering balance."

"Oh." The old man glanced around. "I'm sorry for your loss. It seems like a nice little place."

"Second chances are both bright and terrible things," I told him. He didn't understand and gave me a strange look and left.

I sighed and glanced at my watch. It was near closing time and my back was telling me I'd been standing on this rubber mat, making batter, pouring pancakes, and flipping them for far too long.

"Want me to flip the sign?" Az asked.

"Just do it," Zee called.

I didn't say anything but poured another round of pancakes. I added cinnamon swirl for all of us and then cracked some eggs. Three more plates stacked high with pancakes. One with no toppings. One with far too many toppings. And one that most would consider just right.

The fools.

I took a bite. "They aren't as good as they should be."

"We need help," Zee said. "I've talked to Nathaniel Blake. He'll be on time. He needs the money for school next fall, and it'll give me time to scope out someone better."

I raised my brows, considered objecting, then shrugged.

"Tara took a plea deal. It was generous," Zee said.

I stopped chewing. I'd been waiting to hear but was afraid to ask.

"She'll be in for a while, but with good behavior, it won't be so long. They gave her special circumstances based off of the recent hormonal changes, the betrayal and loss, and the spontaneous nature of it all."

I took a deep breath. "Then we better add another shift and stay open later. She'll need the work when she comes back."

Zee smiled for a moment at that. "You'll be the one on insulin if you keep eating like that. How's your brother, Az?"

"Fine for now," Az said.

I cocked my head at Zee. "You took his file, didn't you?"

"Of course I did. My grandkids live far away, my children are worthless. You all are my family."

I smiled at that and bumped my glass with hers. The Bloody Mary had been made heavy with vodka, but that was what happened when I let Zee make them.

"You hear from Simon?"

I shook my head.

"You're gonna have to get that boy a pint of vanilla ice cream and apologize," Zee said. "Wear something low-cut. You got a nice rack on you."

I leaned back to gasp, but Az nudged me. When I looked at him, he jerked his head towards the door where Simon was waiting outside.

"Speak of the devil," Zee said. She took a sip of her Bloody Mary.

"Go on," Az said in that deep voice of his. "I got Daisy."

I took a deep breath and stood up slowly.

"Don't forget to use your rack," Zee said and then broke into hacking chuckles.

My cheeks were, I was sure, vibrant red when I opened the door and slipped outside to join Simon.

"Hey," I said, taking in his kind eyes.

I very much liked the smile he gave me next, though. "Hey."

I cleared my throat and glanced around, catching Paige from the boutique staring at us through her display window.

I nodded my head towards the ocean. He followed my gaze and we started walking, side by side but not touching.

"You hear about Tara?"

I nodded.

"It was the best I could do," he said.

I pressed my lips together before I spoke. "She killed that idiot. Society can't just let that go. Even if we'd have wanted to do the same."

Simon seemed to relax a little and I realized that he might be anxious too.

"I missed you," I told him, hoping that wasn't too pushy and that I was about to join his long string of ladies.

"I missed you too," he said, sounding surprised.

"I..." We said at once.

"Ladies first," he said.

I did *not* want to go first. But I supposed I could.

"I'm sorry. I shouldn't have texted only Zee. I really did go to talk to Az and get Daisy."

"I know," Simon said. "I saw Daisy there. I knew you didn't have her before. And just because you didn't message me first doesn't mean you wouldn't have."

I felt a flood of relief at that.

"I had to stay away from you. Roberta was watching everything I was doing."

"You dated her," I guessed.

"Yeah," he said, sounding disgusted.

"Sucks she's your boss," I said, laughing.

"Yeah," he agreed. But then he let his hand bump mine, and I looked over. I held out my hand, and he took it, wrapping it up in such utter warmth and strength. We walked the last few blocks in silence and reached the ocean. It was a cool and windy afternoon. The beach was mostly deserted except for a woman and a kid in parkas. Two small dogs ranged around them, never going too far.

I took in a deep breath and caught the scent of salty sea air and the smell of coming rain. I'd go to sleep to the sound of raindrops against my window—a fate I very much looked forward to.

"I was wondering, Rosemary Baldwin," Simon said, distracting me from the rain, "if you'd like to have dinner with me?"

The wind whipped around us, through my hair, and I felt as though I'd experienced this moment before. Or maybe it was just this feeling. This dawning light of a second chance between him and me. I thought I'd ruined things when I hadn't heard from him since Tara had been arrested.

I smiled. "I'd like that very much."

"Seven?"

I nodded again. He leaned closer to me, slowly, giving me plenty of time to dodge. But I didn't. When he kissed me, the wind whipped around both of us and the gentle drizzle of a Pacific Northwest rain began.

Neither of us minded.

The END

Thanks so much for reading my story! If you enjoyed it, I would be so grateful for a review. Reviews mean a lot to writers like me as well as to readers.

THE SEQUEL TO THIS BOOK, COOKIES AND CATASTROPHE IS currently available.

The 2nd Chance Diner is ready for Christmas! Rose has taken up knitting and has produced scarfs enough for half the town. The windows are painted with fake snow, the menu has added pumpkin and peppermint in all their forms. They're even having a Christmas cookie bake-off.

Things take a sinister turn when one of the bakers turns up dead. Was it the competition run amok? Was it some secret crime underbelly of Silver Falls? Maybe the gossip is off, and it was just a terrible accident?

Rose decides that she won't have another event at her diner ruined and decides to investigate. With the snarky Zee in tow, the two of them gossip their way through the murder while trying to avoid Rose's budding romance—the detective who wants neither of them involved.

Order here.

I ALSO HAVE A NEW 1920S COZY HISTORICAL SERIES WHICH HAS been *so much fun* to write. If that's your kind of thing, keep on flipping for the first chapter.

Christmas 1922.

Violet Carlyle--along with a slew of relatives--is called to spend the holidays with their aunt, Agatha Davies. The intransigent woman has spent the majority of her life squirreling away money and alienating her family.

It's hardly the first time Vi has spent the holidays with her aunt. She and her twin intend to do what they always do. Enjoy Aunt Aggie's luxuries while ignoring the histrionics of the family trying to worm their way into the will.

Only this time, Aunt Aggie claims someone is trying to kill her. But how can that be true? Before Vi can find the killer, Aunt Aggie dies. Since Agatha never named an heir, why would anyone want to kill her?

To her shock, Vi finds herself embroiled in a murder investigation where she and her family are the suspects. Just who murdered Aunt Agatha? And why? Will they be able to find the killer before someone else dies?

Order Here.

If you want book updates, you could follow me on Facebook.

MURDER & THE HEIR PREVIEW

"**D**o you really have an appointment so early, Vi?"

"Indeed, dear one," she said, taking the two pills from Giles and the rather noxious concoction that should shake the last of her after-effects from the previous evening.

"We have a letter from Aunt Agatha," Vic told her with a bit of a plea.

"It is your turn to answer for us, darling," Vi said, "I have to deal with our stepmother. She offered me a few things I needed for my wardrobe along with a dress for some party she'll expect me to do the pretty at while I attend and pretend to be good."

"Ahhh, she's persuaded some bloke to *take* a look at you," he laughed.

Violet took up the concoction, drained it in several swallows, and shuddered. Her brother, spoiled soul that he was, never suffered from overindulgence. As his twin, she objected strenuously.

"Must you, darling? I am always certain whenever I answer Aunt Agatha that I've been cross-examined and found wanting."

"Dearest darling," Vi said, taking up her teacup as though it were from the gods' own table, "Stepmother is far easier to deal with if you give her what she wants when it doesn't matter and slip away at the opportune moment. Better to feed the bear than to make her rabid."

"I don't think you become rabid from not eating," Vic mused, filling his plate with kedgeree and toast.

Violet shuddered and pushed the kedgeree farther away her. "Perhaps not. I am not quite up to verbally sparring yet, luv."

"Well, I'll deal with Aggie and see you here for tea? I have dinner plans with Martha Landsy. Would you like to come?"

"I have dinner plans of my own, Victor dear. I'll see what the old battle axe has planned for you, shall I? Then perhaps we should look at escaping London after the New Year and before Stepmother gets too many plans in the works."

"Running scared from the fella ready to give you the look over?"

"There's no shame in a well thought out retreat."

⚘

BUYING DRESSES WITH HER STEPMOTHER WAS EXACTLY WHAT VI thought it would be. She was told that she was getting too old to expect anyone to marry her and she couldn't expect Victor to support her forever. As though Vi didn't contribute to their rooms and living. If her stepmother only knew half the truth, she might leave Violet be, but Vi believed in keeping her cards close to her chest.

"I can only do so much for you, Violet," the battle axe said.

"Yes, Stepmother." Vi adjusted the cloche hat in the mirror and nodded to the dress shop girl, adding several pairs of stockings to her pile.

Lady Eleanor's gaze sharpened on the stockings but she didn't say a word. They'd already discussed her dress choices and her inexplicable demand for an education wherein she hadn't bothered to find a young man from a good family.

"I would think after all this time you could remember to call me mother. You know how your father feels about it."

"Of course," Violet said, refusing to use the word.

Stepmother sniffed and then said, "You and Victor are going to Agatha's for Christmas?"

"Yes, ma'am." Violet nodded to the kid gloves, and the shop girl winked and slid them into the pile without her stepmother even taking note.

"She has a lot of money, Violet. Make yourself useful to her. Victor barely has enough to live on as it is. If he wants to marry, he'll need you gone and something more."

Violet didn't bother rehashing that their father had rather enough money for both Violet and Victor. They each had inherited money from their grandfather, their mother, and had an allowance from their father. Victor would, however, get more money when he turned twenty-five and Violet would receive something when she married. Neither of them were hard-up, so the melodramatics about Violet becoming an old maid had another purpose.

Violet smiled winningly at the shop girl and turned to examine Lady Eleanor. She was a lovely creature.

"Look, Violet," Stepmother said, "I am trying to do my best by you. You know that. Isolde is going off to university, and she's going because she wants to meet a good young man. Surely you don't think that you'll ever marry if Isolde beats you to the altar? My dear, she is *five* years younger than you."

Violet could feel a pulsing at her temples that didn't ease with the pile of lovely things.

"Violet? I am talking to you."

The shop girl winced and then placed an embroidered silk scarf on the pile for Violet along with another pair of stockings. Her step-mother didn't even notice. Violet tapped the counter where a very long strand of jet beads was artfully laid out.

"It is possible given Isolde's wants as compared to my own," Violet said, drawing attention to herself while the shop girl put the beads on Violet's pile of things, "That she might marry before myself. That is the desire of her heart, not mine."

"It should concern you," Stepmother hissed. "You will be *on the shelf.* You'll have to *work* to support yourself when Victor gives up supporting you. He will, Violet."

"Victor?" Vi asked.

Lady Eleanor trod over Violet's insertion and said, "He will marry and he will need to take care *of his wife!*"

Violet sniffed once and said to the shop girl, "I think we've got all we need. Thank you for your help. You can send the bill to Carlyle house and the items to the address I gave you."

Violet turned to her stepmother and tried to avoid an utter breach. "Lady Eleanor, thank you for caring."

"Of course I care," she said, nodding in agreement of Violet's instructions. "I'm *trying* to do what's best for you."

"You are," Violet agreed gently. "It's just that it's not your day any longer, and I am not you or Isolde. I am not going to marry whichever semi-decent man you throw in my path."

"Then what *will* you do?"

"I suppose, if it comes to it, I'll work." Violet enjoyed her stepmother's wince too much.

"Work?" Lady Eleanor pressed her hand to her chest and backed away.

"I will not be the first woman who chooses to support herself rather than marry someone I don't care for. Not even if that man is rolling in the green."

"Working isn't a game, Violet! You are spoilt! And that is your problem. These modern young things who think they know better than their elders. There is quite a lot to be said for a comfortable home and a man who puts you above all others. Whatever will you do to work?"

"I don't know," Violet admitted. "Lila writes magazine articles. Perhaps something like that. I could be a typist, I suppose. I have a friend who takes photographs. I'm sure I can come up with something."

"Your father will be hearing of this," Lady Eleanor hissed, sweeping from the shop.

Violet turned to the shop girl. "I think this means that I need to add that shawl there. And perhaps a few more pairs of stockings. They do go so quickly."

"She's awful," the girl said and then blushed, glancing behind her to ensure no one else had heard.

"Mmmm," Violet said, raising her brows in agreement. Lady Eleanor wasn't quite the worst. She wanted things her way, certainly. As much as Violet despised that, Eleanor also wanted Violet safe and cared for.

"Maybe you could design dresses. There's a squire's daughter who does that," the girl said. She brought Violet over to a champagne pink gown and said, "She made this. She sells through our shop and another in Paris."

Violet ooohed and checked the watch pinned her jacket and then said, "I think I've got time to try that beauty on."

"Will you really get a job?" the girl asked.

Vi supposed the idea of being able to afford to live without working was ridiculous to someone in a shop.

She shrugged and then admitted, "If I wanted to stay in London and Vic really did throw me out. Only my brother would never, ever do that. Besides, he's barely twenty-three. I might be old to get married, but he's too young."

MURDER AND THE HEIR PREVIEW
CHAPTER 2

"Hullo, hullo, hullo, Vi darling, is that you?"

Violet spun around with a grin on her face and tucked a few strands of hair behind her ear. Her gaze fixed upon the bright cheeks and perfectly shingled hair and they both squealed like school girls.

"Gwennie!"

They rushed each other like the chums they were and didn't quite kiss. Carefully applied lipstick could be smudged so easily.

"Gwennie! Whatever are you doing here? Weren't you bouncing around Scotland with your mum?"

She shook her head and her blonde hair flew with the movement. Her bright brown eyes flashed with irritation and her nose crinkled as she said, "My aunt Gertie! It was awful. She's a stern old thing and I spent rather too much time embroidering seat cushions."

Vi winced and squeezed Gwennie's hand before tucking it into the crook of her arm and said, "But you're here now? You've escaped!"

"Thank goodness. Good old Lila and Denny offered to let me come and stay with them for a while when they heard I was ready to throw myself from the highest tower to find an inch of freedom. So I legged it and here I am!"

"And your aunt..." Vi trailed off. She might not have seen Gwennie in simply ages, but she remembered the tune. Gwennie's Aunt Gertrude held the purse strings for Gwennie and did not believe in modern girls. She objected to dancing, drinking, playing cards, and anything that wasn't entirely Victorian.

"Well," Gwennie said in an aside, "She doesn't *love* that I'm here. But Lila is from *such a good family.* And, of course, she and Denny are married. So, Gertie thinks that they'll throw me in the way of dashing and well-connected lads. Perhaps with a touch of a fortune."

Vi winced. Gertrude couldn't be more wrong about Lila and Denny. Most of their friends were starving artists or people Gwennie already knew.

Gwennie raised her brows and said, "She thinks Denny's friends must be matrimonially inclined since he was."

Vi choked at that. Matrimonially inclined? Denny's friends? She laughed. He and Lila had been besotted since they were in the nursery. Their marriage was as fated as the rising sun and they hadn't seen the need to wait.

As far as marriage went, Vi had been hearing that same horrid tune from her stepmother, Lady Eleanor. Thankfully, with Victor's support and her own small inheritance, Vi wasn't quite at daggers drawn with her stepmother. It was getting awfully near to hand as she got older. If Vi went to one more family dinner with some eligible cove sitting by ready to consider her, she might go stark raving mad. It was as though they appeared assuming she was theirs for the taking and all they needed to do was decide whether she'd do. No one seemed to think she deserved to be anything other than grateful.

"Whatever are you doing for tea, darling?" Vi asked, "Would you like to nip home for a bit of something with Vic and I? Vic has found the most wonderful man to help us; I'm sure it'll be scrumptious. Shall we ring up Lila and Denny and bring them along?"

"Oh, that does sound lovely. To get the old girls together. Do you ever miss the school days?"

"Never," Vi admitted. "I was grateful to Aunt Agatha for letting me go to college. You know my father and stepmother expected me to meet someone and marry. Dear Aunt Agatha wanted me to be educated. Not wanted. Expected. You know, the old girl made me write to her about what I was learning and whatnot. Vic and I both, since she paid for him too."

Gwennie laughed and then said, "I wish my aunt was a bit more like yours."

"Well, Aggie was something of a firebrand in her day. Still is, come to think of it."

❧

"WHAT'S ALL THIS THEN?" VIC ASKED AS HE CAME INTO THE drawing room where they were lounging with their tea.

"Hullo, Vic!" Vi called. "You remember Lila and Denny and of course, Gwennie."

He glanced around the room, nodded, and simply slid into one of the sitting chairs.

"Vic! Whatever is the matter?" Vi asked as she poured him a stiff coffee, bypassing the tea she knew he didn't want and making him a plate of biscuits and cake.

"I can't eat darling," he said. "It's too, too bad. We shall need to leave at once. Well..."

"At once? But we have dinner plans and our friends are here."

He groaned and then said, "Well, not at once. In the morning, it's Aggie. The old bean has demanded we appear early. For an *extended* house party with the relatives."

"What?" The twins had planned to head to their aunt's home for Christmas, but that wasn't for a fortnight. Perhaps a long weekend. Maybe a few days longer if the rest of the relatives fled quickly. "No."

"Indeed. She sounded rather weak and washy, too. Simply threw herself upon us to come and rescue her."

"She couldn't have," Vi said.

"She did, I tell you. She did. I read the letter and it was as clear as day."

"But...I don't want to go for a fortnight plus the hols," Vic said, shoving his plate of biscuits back into his lap. She knew him rather well, and when he was hungry he was a bit of a wilting flower. She shook her head at him and headed back across the room to her seat.

"It's worse than you know," he moaned, shoving a whole biscuit into his mouth and talking around it. "She's invited everyone. And she sent a telegraph as well. It came after you left."

Vi blinked, turning slowly back to her brother, shaking her head.

"Indeed. She has. All of them."

"But..."

"Yes," he said, flatly draining his coffee and then rubbing his stomach as though he shouldn't have.

"No."

"It's true," he said weakly. "I saw Algernon at the club when the telegraph arrived. He's got one too, and he's bringing a friend. Possibly two."

"Oh no," Vi said as she dropped into her seat. "Not..."

"Theodophilus? Yes."

Vi shivered. Their cousin Algernon was a blighter. But his friends were worse. Somehow Algernon gave them the impression that he was close to Vi and Vic and that she was up for grabs. Everyone knew that her father would settle a lump of green on her when she married. Algernon seemed to think it was his to half-offer her and the money to his friends.

"I won't do it," Vi said flatly.

"It's Aggie."

Vi bit her lip, glancing at her friends who were watching the exchange with hawk eyes.

"Did you say that Algie is bringing a friend or two?"

"Yes, darling. Asking again won't change things."

"Then we will too." Vi looked at her friends and said, "You're conscripted."

"Oh, but..."

"Rally round, darlings. We need you." She tapped her cheek and then the most enchanting thought occurred to her. "On the way back, we'll swing through Paris and have a lovely time for a few days. Isn't Tomas in Paris? Didn't he say he rented that big house, Vic?"

"Tomas is in love with you, Vi."

"Then he won't object to our arrival."

"Rather mercenary of you, luv," Vic said. "We'll need something to look forward to if we have to spend so long with Algie and the other blood-suckers."

"Mmmm." Vi turned her gaze to her friends. "Please? Please darlings? It won't be all bad. There's a pond for skating and Aggie isn't cheap when it comes to the vittles. She's a mouthy old thing and can be trusted to not control our every move. We could dance some, listen to music, see a bit of the countryside if the weather isn't too bad."

"Denny can you take that much time off?"

"Ah…"

"Paris. Booze. Skating?" Vi wheedled, glancing at Lila who turned her big eyes on her love with a pleading look.

He hemmed and hawed before he said, "I really only half-work anyway. Just enough to keep the pater happy that I'm doing something and keep my allowance coming."

"Then it's resolved! Motion carried. All for one and one for all," Vi laughed.

"This calls for drinks," Victor said, but Vi scowled at him and waved hers away. She had a firm policy of never drinking while she was still struggling with the headache from the last round.

Giles came into the sitting room with another tray of sandwiches and said, "Your new things have arrived, miss."

"Lovely," Vi said. "Come, darlings, and see what I earned this morning."

"What did Eleanor say about me?" Vic asked rather anxiously as Vi rose.

"That your eventual wife would throw me out and I'd have to marry or slum it."

Vic laughed at that and Vi led the girls to her room where Lila threw herself on the bed and Gwennie started to dig through the bags that had arrived.

"You simply robbed her blind, Vi," Gwennie said, as she pulled out the stack of stockings.

"It's not quite so simple as that. Father won't give me an allowance without strings, but he'll still pay for clothes," Vi said. "I just bought rather more than Eleanor realized. Father won't object when he gets the bill. He doesn't get all that many bills from me. I always look like the economical sister because Isolde goes ham."

"Oh, that *is* nice," Gwennie said. "I wish my parents or aunt would do the same. Rather than letting me buy clothes, they simply buy a dress they approve of here or there. Or gift me with a new hat. I get stockings money and not enough for much more. I have to beg for cigarettes."

"Money is the string they use to get us to do what they want us to do," Lila said, "It doesn't get better after you are married. Denny and I get quiet little questions about babies. My mother can't imagine that I might be doing anything to prevent a baby and I don't think Father is even aware that such things exist. They're both quite concerned that I'm barren and Denny will leave me."

"There's time left for babies," Gwennie said, holding up the pink champagne dress against herself. "This is divine."

"It is," Vi agreed. "Thank you for coming with us. The relatives really are rather vile. Aunt Agatha is a doll. An armed and slightly mad doll, but a doll all the same. And you never know who will be with Aunt Agatha. Anything from a painter Lady Eleanor would find objectionable to some rich duke's son."

"That sounds interesting," Lila admitted. "Better than withering away at home while Denny pretends to work."

"It sounds about a million times better than slowly dying with my aunt in Scotland."

"Darlings," Vi said, rising smoothly and adjusting her cuffs. "I'm without a maid, so I'll be having to pack while we chat since Harold Lannister has tickets for *So This is London* and I very much want to go."

"You're wearing this, I hope," Gwennie said, nudging the dress.

Vi smirked and nodded, holding the dress against her body and twirling so it flew out. "Why else would I buy it?"

"Is Harold Lannister rich?" Lila demanded.

"Is he handsome?" Gwennie touched the dress almost longingly.

"He's—witty. Educated. Not ugly, but not handsome. And very, very rich."

"Is he connected to the right families?" Lila asked, channeling Lady Eleanor.

"He's American," Vi said with a wicked grin. "Lady Eleanor would despise him."

ALSO BY BETH BYERS

The Violet Carlyle Historical Mysteries

Murder & the Heir

Murder at Kennington House

Murder at the Folly

A Merry Little Murder

Murder Among the Roses

Murder in the Shallows

Gin & Murder

Murder at the Ladies Club

Weddings Vows & Murder

A Jazzy Little Murder

Murder By Chocolate

The Poison Ink Mysteries

Death by the Book

Death Witnessed

Death by Blackmail

Death Misconstrued

Deathly Ever After

The 2nd Chance Diner Mysteries

Spaghetti, Meatballs, & Murder

Cookies & Catastrophe

Poison & Pie

Double Mocha Murder

Cinnamon Rolls & Cyanide

Tea & Temptation

Donuts & Danger

Scones & Scandal

Lemonade & Loathing

Wedding Cake & Woe

Honeymoons & Honeydew

The Pumpkin Problem

The Brightwater Bay Mysteries

(co-written with Carolyn L. Dean and Angela Blackmoore)

A Little Taste of Murder

(found in the Christmas boxset, The Three Carols of Cozy Christmas Murder)

A Tiny Dash of Death

A Sweet Spoonful of Cyanide

Made in the USA
Middletown, DE
04 September 2019